LILY XIAO SPEAKS OUT

Also by Nicole Chen
It's Boba Time for Pearl Li!

LILY XIAO SPEAKS OUT

NICOLE CHEN

Quill Tree Books
An Imprint of HarperCollinsPublishers

Quill Tree Books is an imprint of HarperCollins Publishers.

www.harpercollinschildrens.com

Library of Congress Control Number: 2023943320
ISBN 978-0-06-332945-4

Typography by Kathy H. Lam and Celeste Knudsen
24 25 26 27 28 LBC 5 4 3 2 1
First Edition

For every reader who's ever felt invisible, may you embrace your inner rocker and speak out, because the world needs to hear what you have to say

CHAPTER
1

IT'S WHEN I REALLY FOCUS on the guitar riffs pounding through my headphones that I can imagine it best. Me, Lily Xiao, under bright stage lights, electric guitar in hand, pouring my heart into a mic and rocking out without a care in the world. I croon another verse, my voice gravelly and my long black hair plastered on my cheeks. Behind me, my best friend and cousin, Vivian, bows her head as her drumsticks fly over the snares. We end the song at exactly the same time, me with one last power strum of the strings, Vivian with a final pound of her cymbals. I let the chords echo through the air, then flick my guitar pick into the cheering audience. Vivian and I grin at the hoots of the crowd, joined together in one last outburst of emotion.

Riiiinnnggg!

My eyes pop open and squint against the California sun bouncing off the cars in the Pacific Park Middle School parking lot.

Yeah, that's about right. A bunch of empty cars is probably the closest to a real rock audience I'll ever get—not to mention have the guts to jam out in front of.

Kids start to stream past me and down the school steps to get to the bike racks below. It's Friday afternoon, which means most kids book it out of here pretty quick so they can do fun stuff together, like walk to the mall for some shopping or bike to 7-Eleven for blue raspberry Slurpees.

I don't have a clique to hang out with, though. My parents would rather I head straight home to do homework. But Fridays are my open days, when I'm allowed to do anything I want to after school, like go to my favorite place in the whole wide world, Power Records.

Suddenly, someone bumps up against my purple backpack, knocking it down a few steps. My tattered copy of *The Westing Game* tumbles out.

"Hey, watch it!" I scramble after my stuff and glare into the sea of baggy jeans.

But whoever it was doesn't bother turning their head to say sorry. Or toss me an apologetic look.

Scowling, I grab *The Westing Game* before it gets trampled on, dust it off, and slide it gently back into my bag.

It was actually pretty cool that Mr. Silvers let our English literature class out early so we could get an early start on the chapters he'd assigned for the weekend. Reading outside in the sun is way better than in the classroom, where the fluorescent lights buzz like nervous mosquitos. But I decided to listen to music instead of reading, because I finished the entire book three days ago.

I'm Lily Xiao, class robot, after all.

At least that's what someone scribbled into my 1991–1992 Pacific Park Middle School yearbook at the end of sixth grade last year: *Have a good summer, Lily. Hope our class robot changes its programming and does something cool and different for once!*

I have no idea who wrote it, which made it hurt more. It could be any one of these kids jogging past me who thinks I'm some boring Goody-Two-shoes who does whatever she's told.

Or worse, it could be everyone who thinks that.

Whatever. Pearl Jam, the coolest grunge rock band in the world, couldn't care less about other people's opinion of them. I read in a magazine that they even showed up at a fancy award show once in flannel shirts and ripped jeans to make a statement about elitism in the music industry.

What's wrong with getting schoolwork done early, anyway? It frees up time to do better things, like listen to the most amazing music ever while soaking in rays on a Friday afternoon.

Fun fact: Pacific Park's slogan is "Climate Best by Government Test." Apparently, based on meteorological tests done in the 1920s, Pacific Park beat some Mediterranean island and a city in North Africa to earn the title.

It'd help the vibe I'm aiming for if it wasn't so nice all the time, though. No wonder grunge rock came from Seattle, where the weather matches the dark, gloomy energy of the music.

At least it's cool enough today that the red flannel shirt I'm wearing over my heather-gray T-shirt isn't making me sweat like a broken, drippy sprinkler. Plus, the sun makes my new black patent leather boots shine just right.

I'm not in a real grunge band yet. But fake it till you make it, right?

I stand up and scan the crowd for Vivian's purple-and-green jacket. She's nowhere to be seen, so I plop back down and put on my headphones again. I push the Play button on my Discman, and it vibrates slightly as the CD inside starts to spin.

Stone Gossard, the band's rhythm guitarist, kicks off Pearl Jam's "Alive" with an electrifying slide of the strings. After a few riffs, Mike McCready and Jeff Ament's pounding lead and bass guitars join him, and

Dave Krusen's percussion pumps up the intensity. Then Eddie Vedder launches into his guttingly deep vocals.

Every time I hear my favorite grunge rock band play, I get chills. Their sound isn't like anything that plays on the radio, which is usually bright and happy in a kind of fake, manufactured way. Instead, Pearl Jam is rich and soulful. Eddie Vedder sings with such passion and power that it blows me away every time he opens his mouth.

What's cool, too, about Pearl Jam is that they sound nothing like how they look. If the whole band walked by me on the street, I wouldn't notice they were famous. They're just some guys with long hair in flannel shirts and baggy pants.

But when they pick up their instruments and get up onstage, they turn into something incredibly raw and brave.

I would give anything for the guts to transform like they do.

Suddenly something pokes me from behind, and a wave of annoyance rises from my chest.

Not again.

This time, though, Pearl Jam's rocker vibes have had enough time to course through my veins. I rip off my headphones and twist backward to confront the poking offender.

Robot: engage attack mode. Beep boop bop.

"Ha ha, shì wǒ!" Purple and green flash in front of me, and Vivian's big anime eyes twinkle at me from behind her long bangs.

"Nǐ zài gàn shén me?" I whine in Mandarin Chinese, half laughing. "That hurt!" I rub my arm and pout, sticking my lower lip out like when we were little kids and I'd beg her to let me have the last pineapple cake.

Vivian reaches out her hand and pulls me to my feet. "Aw, you're fine," she continues in Mandarin. "You're my biǎo jiě, aren't you? You can take a little poke."

"Hey, I'm only two months older. That doesn't mean my bones are any stronger than yours," I say, brushing off any leftover dust from my poor backpack before hoisting it over my shoulders.

"Well, it still counts." She pouts back.

"At least my skin is thicker." I yank on her sleeve. "Take off this jacket! You need to get used to the weather here."

Vivian shivers. "But it's so cold compared to Taipei."

I roll my eyes, but I can't hold back my giggles. "You've been living here for nearly six months now. Nǐ xiàn zài yīng gāi xí guàn le."

Vivian's English isn't very good, so the two of us talk in Chinese when we're together, even when we're at school. It's probably not the best thing—no one else understands, and sometimes we get dirty looks when we break out laughing and nobody else knows why.

But it's hard for Vivian to get by all day in English, and my Chinese is pretty good after spending every summer in Taipei since I was four. So I try to make it easy for her when we're together.

That's what cousins are for, right? To help each other, no matter what.

Plus, it's kind of nice to have a secret language that only the two of us understand.

"Sorry I'm late getting out of class. I had to check in with Mr. Silvers about the reading assignment," Vivian says as we skip down the steps and head toward our bikes. "What are you listening to?" she asks, pointing at the Discman in my hands.

"Nǐ cāi." I tell her to guess, grinning back at her knowingly.

Vivian rolls her eyes. "You're listening to Pearl Jam again, right?"

"Dāng rán!" I stick out my tongue at her as I twist the black knob on my bike lock. "Who else?"

"Let me hear." She puts on my headphones and starts bouncing to the pounding rhythm.

As I pull my bike free from the steel racks, I glance around. There are still a few kids scattered about, but the biggest group left is a crowd of boys in baggy pants and long-sleeved shirts on the opposite corner of the parking lot. Music blares from a boombox, and three of them take turns kicking at a hacky sack while a few others jump off the edge of the sidewalk with their skateboards. One boy is doing lazy figure-eight loops on the concrete.

Skateboards and boomboxes aren't allowed on campus. There's a big sign in the front that says so.

Skater boys seem to love breaking the rules, though.

When I hear a pause in the music, I nudge Vivian again. "You don't need to go to the library again today, do you, biǎo mèi?"

Vivian pulls off the headphones and hands them back to me. "I should probably keep studying."

"Aw, it's Friday!" I groan. "You can take a break, can't you?"

"I don't know. I'm so behind in my reading." Her face looks worried as she slips her bright pink bike helmet over her short hair.

"Come on, puh-lease?" I stick my lower lip out again. "Let's do something fun together."

Vivian hesitates. "I don't know. I should get home."

"Look at this." I pull out a crinkled ten-dollar bill from my pocket and wave it in the air. "Ah-ma gave me this yesterday because of the A I got on that super-difficult algebra problem set. Let's go to Power Records and spend it."

Vivian sighs. "Okay, for a little bit."

"Hooray!" I hop onto my bike and start pedaling in the direction of my favorite record store in Pacific Park.

A trip to Power Records will definitely erase Vivian's worries.

Or drown them out with a loud rock song.

CHAPTER 2

WALKING INTO POWER RECORDS ALWAYS takes my breath away. After we push through the glass doors, my eyes take a few seconds to adjust to the buzzing fluorescent lights. Then the aisles and shelves stocked and stacked with a never-ending number of CDs and records come into view.

So.

Much.

Music.

The store is packed as usual for a Friday afternoon. A group of college students mill around the Billboard Top 40 display, and a pair of girls dressed in flowery baby-doll dresses make their way upstairs, where there's a second floor of music goodness and a small café where you can have coffee and smoothies. Sprinkled throughout the aisles are people flipping through bins filled with CD cases or standing at listening stations, headphones on and jamming out to whatever music they're thinking of buying. There's even a woman waving her arms around with her eyes closed like an orchestra conductor.

I love seeing people so into their thing. That's the best part about Power Records—it's the kind of place where it doesn't matter who you are or what you look like.

What matters is that you love music.

I beeline it for the grunge rock section along the back wall, and Vivian follows me as I zigzag between aisles.

When we get closer, I see Keiko sitting cross-legged on the concrete floor, slotting CDs onto shelves. Her dark hair is tied up in two loose buns, and she's wearing a pair of baggy overalls over a black tank top that has a smiley face traced in yellow with Xs for eyes and the word "Nirvana" scribbled on it.

Keiko's the only person I know who plays in a real rock band. When she's not working at Power Records, she goes to the community college here in Pacific Park. But her dream is to make music. She's the lead guitarist of her band, and her girlfriend, Joan, sings vocals.

Keiko doesn't have to fake grunge like I do. Sometimes I wonder how she got as cool as she is. And if she'd be able to teach me one day.

Keiko waves hello as we approach. "Hey, Lily! Hey, Vivian! How's it going?"

I point at her shirt. "Nirvana, huh?"

Nirvana is all the rage these days. Their music videos are always playing on MTV, especially that one where they're headbanging in a high school gym and there's a wrinkled old janitor cleaning up after them.

Personally, I like the deeper, introspective style of Pearl Jam more. Nirvana's punk sound is a little too . . . frantic . . . for me. But they're pretty good, and I have their album *Nevermind* at home.

"Yeah, I caught them in concert a few weeks ago. They were out of this world!" Keiko blows a strand of black hair away from her face.

"Wow, how cool! A real concert, huh?" I exclaim.

Vivian speaks up in English. "What is . . . what you say . . . concert?"

I quickly translate what Keiko said into Mandarin. "Tā qù le yī chǎng yáo gǔn yīn yuè huì. Nirvana dé."

Vivian's eyes light up and she starts bouncing up and down like an excited puppy. "Wǒ yě xiǎng qù! Keiko, where we buy door tickets?"

I don't want to embarrass my cousin, so I hold back my giggle. But it's adorable how Vivian gets the English translation of "concert ticket" slightly wrong. In Mandarin Chinese, we'd say "mén piào" if we wanted to go to a concert, and "mén" means "door" and "piào" means "ticket."

Vivian knows enough English to get by, but she still

makes mistakes and mixes in Chinese a lot. That doesn't stop her from saying what's on her mind, though, which is more than I can do. And I speak perfect English.

She's the best.

Keiko pauses, probably trying to figure out what Vivian means. So I chime in. "Vivian's asking where we can get concert tickets, Keiko."

"Ah, gotcha. Unfortunately, I think the band's back in Seattle, so no more shows for now."

Vivian's face falls.

"I did sort a new batch of used music earlier today, though," Keiko quickly adds, pointing to the bright yellow bins in the corner.

It's not two tickets to a real concert, but those bins *are* one of my favorite things about the store. You can find great stuff in them and for way cheaper than a brand-new CD. Sometimes, even recently released albums end up in there.

Vivian and I head over and start rummaging through the bins. It's quiet as we focus on pulling out the ones with cool covers and flipping them around to read the song names on the back.

My fingers pause. I pull out a CD and inspect the purple lettering. "Vivian, look! It's the Temple of the Dog's album! I read about them in last month's issue of *Rolling Stone*," I marvel. "This was Eddie Vedder's first recording ever. That guy from Soundgarden, Chris Cornell, invited him to sing, and there were a couple of band members who helped record the album. It was a tribute to a mutual friend of theirs."

Vivian tosses me a thumbs-up. "Get it! We can listen to it together this weekend."

I bring it to Keiko at the counter and hand her Ah-ma's crumpled ten-dollar bill. "I'll take this one."

Keiko slides it into one of Power Records' signature yellow plastic bags. "Good choice. Did you know that this album is the first one Eddie Vedder ever sang on? And that getting together to record it is how Pearl Jam was formed?"

I grin. "I do know."

"Wow, you sure know your music, Lily." Keiko winks at me, and my heart swells.

Maybe I'm more grunge than I think I am.

Suddenly the sound of boys' voices catches my attention. I turn around as four of the skater boys I saw earlier by the school parking lot saunter in.

I recognize Marcos Alvarez right away because of the green backward baseball cap he always wears down low. It squishes the floppy brown hair that covers his dark eyes and thick, soft eyelashes. Marcos and I both went to Oak Elementary, and I remember how every time it rained when we were in the first grade, we'd dash to the corner of the playground by the shed and play bakery together. We'd make and pretend to sell pies full of twigs and pebble chocolate chips to our classmates, pocketing the small change we earned to buy chocolate milk at lunch later.

But that was a long time ago. Now that we're in middle school, staying friends takes a lot more than mud pies. Marcos and I are in the same seventh-period English lit class, but I sit in the front while he sits in the back. Skater boys like him always sit behind everyone else.

The other boys didn't go to Oak Elementary, so I don't know their names.

"Hey, you work here?" Marcos tips his chin up at Keiko while I take a few steps back to shrink behind a shelf of CDs. Vivian stays where she is, though, and stares at the boys with a curious look on her face.

"Sure do," Keiko replies cheerfully. "I'm the rock-and-roll expert around here. How can I help?"

The boy with a red beanie and long blond hair curling around his T-shirt collar snickers. "You like rock music? I thought chicks like you only played the violin or piano or boring music like that."

At his words, my hands clench into tight fists. What is this guy talking about? Is he suggesting that Asians like me and Keiko can only like classical music?

I mean, don't get me wrong, I love a good Haydn or Chopin concerto. But I can love rock music, too. So what if there aren't people who look like me and Keiko in the rock bands that show up on MTV?

I don't see any jerks who look like they're wearing ketchup on their heads on the cable channel that plays the best selection of music videos, either.

Keiko scoffs and shakes her head. "Don't call me a chick. I know more about this type of music than you ever will." She sticks out her chin defiantly. "And stop perpetuating stereotypes, kid."

I can't help but grin. Keiko is grunge outside *and* in.

"So what are you looking for?" she continues, turning toward Marcos and ignoring Ketchup Head.

Marcos shoots his friend a glare. "My buddies and I are totally digging Soundgarden these days. Can you recommend other bands like them?"

Keiko glances at me. "You guys know Lily? She knows a ton about this type of music, too. What do you think, Lily? Any suggestions?"

Like the spotlights at a rock-and-roll concert, all eyes turn toward me.

My mind goes blank.

"Uh, I dunno," I manage to say, my face turning red. I can practically feel their eyes boring into me like a drill. They're probably wondering what another Asian chick is doing here in the grunge section, and not in the classical music section where I belong.

"Actually, uh, I gotta go," I squeak before grabbing the yellow bag with my Temple of the Dog CD from the counter. "Wǒ men yīng gāi huí jiā," I mumble to Vivian, then quickly scoot by the boys with my head down and make my escape.

As I weave between the aisles in the jazz and pop sections before pushing open the glass door to get outside, I groan in my head.

That last chicken move of mine, where I can never talk to other kids from school because I'm afraid of what they'll think of me?

Definitely *not* grunge.

"Hey, děng děng wǒ!" Vivian catches up to me at the bike racks of the shopping plaza. "Why didn't you say something? You could have told them about your new album!" she says, panting.

"I didn't think they'd be interested." I kick the steel racks in frustration.

"Really?" Vivian stares at me with an eyebrow arched high.

"Fine. I'm a big chicken." I pout.

A chicken robot, to be exact. Programmed to be perfect, but malfunctions at the slightest ruffle of my feathers. Especially when threatened.

Vivian's face softens, and she slings her arm around my shoulder. "You're not a chicken, Lily. It's okay to be shy. Once my English is better, I'll turn those kids into our friends."

Vivian doesn't have any friends besides me at Pacific

Park Middle School, but that has more to do with her English than her not being likable. She's way more outgoing than I am and has a ton of friends back in Taiwan. They even send her letters and cute postcards now that she's here. I wish I had friends like that who'd write to me if I moved halfway around the world.

But I have no interest in being friends with those boys. Still, I'm annoyed at myself for not saying anything when Keiko invited me to chime in about cool grunge music.

The sun starts to dip below the brown-tiled roofs of the shopping plaza stores, and I glance at my watch. It's 5:18.

"Hey, I should probably head home. I promised Ah-ma I'd help her with dinner tonight."

"Yeah, I should get home, too." Vivian starts to spin the lock on her bike.

I pull mine up from the rack and clip on my helmet. "You and Auntie and Uncle are coming over for dinner tomorrow night, right?"

"Yep. I'll see you then?"

I nod, and we both hop on our bikes and head in opposite directions.

CHAPTER
3

HOME IS A ONE-STORY CONDO on Grand View Court that looks exactly the same as the other ones it's attached to. You can tell which one is ours, though, from the red paper diamond with the word "富" hanging upside down on our door. Chinese New Year was a few months ago, but Mom decided to leave it up to invite good luck and fortune into the house year-round.

I love how cute and cozy our little condo is. But Mom's always talking about how one day, she hopes we'll be able to afford our own "single family home," with a two-car garage and a backyard.

I'm not sure why we need all that, though. We're a single family that fits into this one already.

When I swing the front door open, Ah-ma's at the

living room table with a huge pile of mung bean sprouts in front of her. I can hear Dad rustling around in the kitchen, probably busy with some cooking-related task that Ah-ma's asked him to do.

When it comes to food, Ah-ma rules the roost in the Xiao household.

She also kind of looks like a rooster, with her hair piled high on her head in a perfect twist. Even the way Ah-ma walks, super straight and dignified, reminds me of the way the birds strut, proud and strong.

"Ah, tsa-bóo-sun," Ah-ma calls out in Taiwanese. "Come and help me." She pats the dark-lacquered wood chair next to her. I tug off my shoes and shuffle into my slippers before taking the seat.

Ugh. Bean sprouts are one of my favorite veggies, with their crispy white, slightly sweet stems. But preparing them takes *forever*. I can't even start to count how many hours I've spent plucking off the ends of a veggie that takes my family five minutes to scarf down once it hits the table.

Ah-ma's fingers fly as she snaps off the stringy end of a sprout and tosses the two pieces into different piles before doing it over again.

"How was school today, Lily?" Ah-ma asks, continuing in Taiwanese.

"Fine. I did well on my biology test," I reply in

Mandarin. I understand Taiwanese, but I can't speak it very well. I usually respond to Ah-ma in Mandarin instead, which she understands perfectly because most people in Taiwan speak both.

"Good. Doing well in school will open doors of opportunity for you. You make this old woman proud." Ah-ma squeezes my arm and smiles at me mischievously.

I giggle. "Aww, you're not an old woman, Ah-ma!"

"Tell that to my tired bones." She sighs dramatically. "How is Vivian?"

I reach for another handful of mung beans. "Fine. We had lunch together, as usual."

"Keep watching out for her, okay? Although you're older, she's the one who took care of you every summer you were in Taipei."

"Yes, Ah-ma, I know," I reply, hoping my tone comes across as appropriately obedient. But sometimes I wish she would stop reminding me. *I'm only older by two months!* I want to shout. That's barely enough time to memorize the lyrics of an entire album. Breathing air for sixty days more than someone else doesn't mean I know more about life than they do.

Still, in Taiwanese culture, age matters a lot. The older someone is, the more respectful you need to be to them. In return, that older person has to watch out for the younger one. Apparently, I have a big debt to repay to my younger cousin for showing me around Taipei for so many summers.

And for being the one who has more guts to speak up than I do.

The fact that I'm older is also why Vivian's parents had her call me "biǎo jiě" when we were little kids, which means "older sister cousin." I call her "biǎo mèi," or "younger sister cousin." And now, those two names have stuck over the years.

"I promise I'm doing my best to watch out for Vivian." I snap a mung bean sprout too hard, and it breaks in half. I sigh and toss both pieces into the throw-away pile. "I even took her to the record store after school."

"Good, good." Ah-ma's voice dips low, and she glances at the kitchen, where my dad is. "Did you buy anything with the money I gave you?"

I hunch over a little deeper, too. "Yes, I got a new album, another grunge one. Well, it wasn't brand-new, but used, which made it cheaper."

"It's always good to be resourceful. I'm glad you got more of this music you like so much." Ah-ma pats my cheek before turning back to the mung beans.

I smile to myself. The only thing Ah-ma knows about grunge rock is that the music is loud and played in front of a screaming crowd by guys in baggy clothes that could use ironing. She accepts my love for it, though, unlike my parents, who only tolerate what they think is a weird taste in music. What matters to them is that it doesn't get in the way of my schoolwork.

Dad walks in from the kitchen, wiping his hands on the flowered apron around his waist. His black rectangle-shaped glasses are slipping down his nose, and he's wearing an aqua-blue polo shirt today.

There's a game I like to play—what shade of blue is Dad's polo shirt today?

Yesterday, it was . . . drum roll . . . navy!

The day before . . . drum roll . . . periwinkle!

"Hey, Lily, welcome home. Ma, I've sliced up the beef like you wanted and it's marinating in the fridge." He pulls back a chair and joins us.

"How was work, Dad?" I ask.

"Great, actually." He snaps the ends off two sprouts at a time. "I came up with an idea for a new way to speed up the data connections we're testing at work. But it's never been done before, and my boss isn't that excited about it."

Dad is a network engineer at CompuScape, a company that makes computers and printers and stuff like that. I'm not totally sure what he does, though. All I know is that it has something to do with getting computers to talk to each other and share information.

Ah-ma tsks. "You and your ideas, son. Be careful you don't get your boss angry."

"Ma." Dad tosses a handful of sprout ends into the

pile. "Don't worry. It's only a thought at this point. I need to do more research to see if it's actually doable. Plus, it wouldn't hurt to rock the boat a bit at work." He catches my eye and winks.

I shrug back at him. Ah-ma's always warning us to be careful and to not get into trouble with people like Dad's or Mom's bosses, my teachers, or anyone remotely connected to the government. Once, our mail got soaked when the mailman didn't shut the mailbox right and it rained. When Mom found out one of the waterlogged envelopes was a paycheck, she started to storm out of the house the second the mail truck pulled up in front of our house the next day to give him a piece of her mind.

But Ah-ma's pleading to "not get us in trouble" and "remember what's happened before" and other stuff I couldn't follow because Ah-ma's Taiwanese was too fast stopped Mom in her tracks. Since then, Mom always greets the mailman with a stiff smile and utter politeness.

Ah-ma's tough, all right, especially when it comes to what she expects of her family. But when it's about things that happen outside our home, she's also kind of . . . afraid.

With Dad's help, we get through the pile of sprouts before my stomach falls out of my body from hunger. Mom comes home from her job as an accountant, and we inhale Ah-ma's dinner in a record fifteen minutes.

Then Mom, Dad, and Ah-ma gather around the TV to watch the next episode of *Sān duǒ huā*, their latest soap opera obsession from Taiwan. Mom gets the tapes every other week at the video rental shop in Sunnydale two towns over. But I make an excuse to skip it and head to my room instead.

I've got new music to listen to.

CHAPTER
4

MY ROOM'S TWO DOORS DOWN from the living room, sandwiched between Mom and Dad's and Ah-ma's, but on the opposite side of the hallway. It's small with boring tan carpet, eggshell-white stucco walls, and a wooden desk shoved in the corner for the all-important task of doing homework.

When we moved to this condo three years ago, right before Ah-ma came to live with us, I begged Dad and Mom to let me paint my bedroom walls a fun color, like teal blue or bright pink. The bedrooms on the TV shows I love watching are always so bright and colorful, with posters on the walls and floral duvets and ruffled pillows nestled on the beds.

But my parents were super nervous about the idea.

"This isn't our own home," Mom said. "I'm not sure we should be messing with it. I don't want to get in trouble with the landlord."

"Couldn't you ask them if it's allowed? I can help paint it back when we move," I had pleaded.

"I don't think that's the best idea," my dad chimed in. "Let's not bother them with things that aren't important."

Being able to make this bedroom my own *was* important, I wanted to argue back. I wanted this room to *feel* like mine, even though it wasn't really.

I bit my tongue, though.

So I've done my best with what I have, putting up posters with tape—not pushpins!—and filling my bookshelves with cute knickknacks like my Hello Kitty and Troll figurines. Half of the shelves hold my collection of Japanese manga, which looks pretty cool with their spines lined up neat and matching.

My books aren't in the original Japanese, though—they're translated into Mandarin Chinese. I don't know a lot about Taiwanese history, but Mom and Dad told me that Japan ruled the island of Taiwan, which is off the east coast of China, for almost fifty years before they had to leave it after losing World War II. That's why a lot of Taiwanese culture has been influenced by Japan, making manga a big deal in both countries. Ah-ma actually speaks Japanese way better than Mandarin because she was born when Japan was still in charge.

My favorite manga series is Xiǎo Dīng Dāng, or Doraemon in Japanese. He's this blue cat robot from the future who comes to help Nobita, a dorky kid who is the great-great-grandfather of Xiǎo Dīng Dāng's owner. Whenever they get into trouble, Xiǎo Dīng Dāng pulls out gadgets from a magical pouch on his belly to solve things. Then they get into even more trouble!

I wish I had a cool cat robot with a magical pouch to be my buddy, too.

I flop onto my red beanbag, the foam beads inside shifting to hug my body. I unzip my backpack and pull out my new-but-used Temple of the Dog CD, then carefully slide my fingernail down the side of the cellophane wrap. After peeling the acetate away, I crack open the jewel case and push down the little button in the middle.

With a satisfying *pop*, the shiny, silvery disc of musical goodness comes loose.

Best.

Feeling.

Ever.

I carefully lift the CD out of its case, doing my best not to leave any fingerprints. I flip it over and hold it up to the light to check for scratches. This is a used product, after all.

Luckily, the surface is as smooth and shiny as Taiwan's Sun Moon Lake.

A quick puff of breath blows any invisible dust specks away. With my free hand, I push the Open/Close button on my stereo. The tray slides open, like it's sticking out its tongue and asking me to feed it.

My silver stereo with shiny mint-green trim is the fanciest thing I own. My parents got it for me when I won "Sixth Grade Student of the Year" last June.

At first, I was super proud of winning. My whole family showed up for the awards ceremony, and seeing them in the crowd and beaming so happily made me stand a bit taller.

But when it was time for me to get up in front of everyone and give my speech, I panicked. My face flushed bright red, my heart pounded a mile a minute, and I got so flustered that I could barely make it the whole way through.

It was a good thing I had memorized what I wanted to say a week before, though. My brain went on automatic mode, and my voice followed.

At least I *thought* it was a good thing.

Later that night, my family watched the video Mom recorded of me giving my speech. I looked so awkward up there, with my voice flat and monotone and my movements jerky and unnatural. My delivery was basically the complete opposite of Pearl Jam's amazing vibe when they perform.

It was horrifying. I could see why someone decided to call me the "class robot."

Mom, Dad, and Ah-ma gushed over how excited they were to see me onstage, though, and surprised me with a brand-new stereo the next morning.

At least I got something out of my misery.

I slip the Temple of the Dog CD into the open tray, lean back into my beanbag chair, and close my eyes. The stereo whirls to life, and after a few seconds, the first guitar strums begin, with a faint cymbal rhythm keeping beat. Chris Cornell's rich voice kicks off "Hunger Strike," slow, calm, controlled. Eddie Vedder joins in the second verse, along with Matt Cameron's drumming . . . building in intensity . . . until the drums kick off full force about halfway through.

It's magic.

The first time I heard grunge rock, I'd just gotten back from my summer in Taipei. It was the middle of the night, and I couldn't sleep. Not only was the jet lag brutal, but I was also feeling sorry for myself. Seventh grade was about to start, and I was *not* looking forward to another year without a best friend by my side.

It's not that I was a total hermit during the sixth grade, with no friends at all. I knew the Oak Elementary kids and got to know a few from the other schools that feed into Pacific Park Middle through group projects or being assigned to sit next to them in class.

But somehow, after the excitement of starting middle school, most of the Pacific Park Middle sixth graders seemed to figure out fast who their new best friends were or formed tight cliques. It was too overwhelming for me, though, and I ended up without anyone to hang out with during recess or lunch. And I had a feeling those friendships got even stronger over the summer while I was away in Taipei with my family. Seventh grade wasn't going to be any better than sixth. So in the middle of that anxious, sleepless night, I turned on the radio to see if some music could calm my restless, nervous brain.

Right away, Eddie Vedder's soulful voice and the band's rich instrumentals started to echo off the walls of my bedroom.

I figured out a few days later that the slow yet powerful rock ballad I'd heard was Pearl Jam's single "Black." To be honest, I still don't understand the lyrics, but the song's vibe made me feel exactly what I needed to in that lonely, gloomy moment. Like no matter how hard things got, it'd end up okay.

And it eventually did, although I didn't know it at the time. Two weeks later, Dad gave me the exciting news that Vivian's mom was given a work visa from the US government and had decided to join me, Dad, Mom, and Ah-ma in making Pacific Park home. My cousin and I could finally be together for longer than a summer! She was going to be on my turf, and I now had someone to hang out with and eat lunch with at school. Whew.

A few days after the night I first heard Pearl Jam on the radio, I read a magazine article about the band. It said that before Eddie joined Pearl Jam, he was working at a gas station in San Diego when Jeff Ament and Stone Gossard, the original band members, heard his demo tape and liked it. So they invited him up to Seattle to record the Temple of the Dog album with Chris Cornell. But Eddie was so shy and awkward at their first meeting that the band wasn't sure he'd be the right singer for them. Then he opened his mouth and let out that powerful voice of his. From that moment on, there was no doubt in their minds that he was the one.

That story cemented in my head how awesome Eddie Vedder is. Somehow, he's figured out how to be a rock star *despite* being shy and awkward.

Thinking about Eddie and his first time with the band makes the image of Keiko asking me—actually, more like inviting me—to tell Marcos about Temple of the Dog flash into my head. I flip around and bury myself into the soft plushness of the beanbag.

Like a cowardly ostrich.

So when Eddie croons over and over again about going hungry in this powerful music that fills every corner of my room, I can't help but feel that same hunger.

A hunger to be as amazing and brave and strong as Eddie is.

Even if I'm shy and awkward, too.

CHAPTER
5

THE MOMENT I BLINK OPEN my eyes the next morning, I hear sizzling sounds coming from the kitchen. I throw off the covers and head out, stomach growling.

Mom is flipping something around in a pan at the stove, and Dad's at the table, reading the Chinese newspaper. His polo today is . . . drum roll . . .

Turquoise!

At the sound of my entrance, Mom turns around and flashes me a big smile. "Morning, Lily."

"Zǎo ān," I chirp back. "Is that what I think it is?"

"You're right on time. I picked up a bunch of cōng yóu bǐngs from Auntie Ying on the way home yesterday. Here, this batch is done." She slides the flat pancake speckled with bits of green onion onto a cutting board and presses a cleaver into it, cutting triangles like a pizza. "Take these to the table, please."

I take the plate and settle next to my dad, then pick up a steaming slice of Taiwanese green onion pancake. They're nice and crispy, with flaky layers that have a great chew to them.

Auntie Ying is famous among the Taiwanese community in Pacific Park for her cōng yóu bǐngs. Once a month, she makes a huge batch from her kitchen, freezes them, and sells them to those in the know.

"By the way, I brought some of these over to your aunt earlier this morning. She says you should call Vivian," Mom says as she presses another disk of dough flat with the palm of her hand.

"Oh, okay!" I jump up and pull the receiver off the phone that's hanging on the kitchen wall. After I hear the dial tone, I press the buttons for the number I've memorized by heart.

Vivian answers right away. "Lily! Will you come with me to the library today? Please, please, pretty please?"

Oh no. Saturday mornings are for relaxing at home and catching up on the TV shows I recorded during the week.

Saturday mornings are *not* about going to the library.

"Aw, Vivian," I groan. "I don't want to study right now. We've got the entire weekend to do that."

"Please, biǎo jiě? It's so lonely sitting there by myself."

Ah-ma walks in, decked out in her sweatsuit and swinging her arms back and forth like she always does after a session of tài jí out on our little condo patio.

Seeing Ah-ma reminds me of my promise that I'd try harder to be a good older-sister-cousin.

"All right, all right, I'll come. Meet you there in a half hour?"

"Yay, thanks, biǎo jiě!" Vivian squeals.

There goes my Saturday.

The things you do for family.

Two hours later, I can't take it anymore. I've already finished a problem set, my grammar worksheets, and written a short essay about the Fourteenth Amendment.

Ah-ma would be so proud. Mom and Dad, too.

Meanwhile, Vivian's still hunched over her copy of *The Westing Game*, stopping every few minutes to flip through her English-Chinese dictionary. My cōng yóu bǐng breakfast feels like it happened forever ago.

"Vivian," I groan. "Can we please take a break? Maybe go outside for a few minutes?" I pretend to shut down. "Beep boop bop. Robot out of battery. Recharge needed ASAP."

Vivian doesn't glance up from her reading. "I want to finish this chapter. But go."

"Are you sure you don't want a break?"

"No, it's fine. In Taipei, we usually go to tutoring

class all day Saturday and Sunday, plus after school on the weekdays. This is nothing," she insists, scribbling something down in her notebook.

I shake my head as I make my way outside. I can't believe she's got energy for so much of this.

Once her English is better, though, Vivian's going to find this a breeze. Then we'll have way more time to geek out about music, instead of being cooped up at the library all day.

The sun feels so nice and warm on my face, and I tilt my head back to let more of that delicious vitamin D shine onto my cheeks. I figure I've got about three songs before I should head back inside. I slide on my headphones and hit Play on the Discman before shoving it into my pocket. Then I start to jog up and down the library steps.

Temple of the Dog's "Say Hello 2 Heaven" starts streaming through my ears, and I try to match my pace to the rhythm of the bass.

That's the stuff. My blood's moving again already.

Robot: charging. Bop boop.

After a few minutes, I'm huffing and puffing. As I catch my breath at the top of the stairs, I skim the posters pinned on the community bulletin board. Might as well see what's shaking in civic news here in Pacific Park.

It's the typical stuff . . . a flyer for babysitting services, some posters about upcoming events, and a placard telling everyone to vote in the local elections.

Then a shiny poster catches my eye. It's got a picture of what looks like a group of kids playing instruments on a stage. I lean in closer—one's strumming an electric guitar while another sits behind a drum set complete with bass, snares, tom-toms, and cymbals. Underneath the photo in big block letters are the words "WANT TO BE A ROCK STAR? SIGN UP FOR CAMP ROCK OUT THIS SUMMER AND WE'LL TEACH YOU!"

I scan the text quickly, my heart pounding with every detail I take in.

At Camp Rock Out, we teach you everything you need to know to start playing electric guitar, drums, bass, keyboards, even to learn vocals! Simply tell us your instrument, and one will be waiting for you on Day 1. After four weeks, you'll be ready to get onstage and rock out in an end-of-camp performance for your family and friends. We provide the stage; you provide the rock vibes! Register by April 16 to secure your spot.

I can't believe it. Is this my chance to get my hands on a real guitar?!

I read the poster again to make sure I'm not seeing things. But my eyes linger on the part about "an end-of-camp performance."

Gulp. It's one thing to daydream about spilling your heart out with a guitar in your arms like Pearl Jam does. But it's another thing to do it in real life.

Could I get up onstage in front of strangers and rock out like Eddie Vedder does? What would people think about someone like me jamming to an electric guitar and belting lyrics into a mic?

No. I couldn't do it. What a silly idea.

Plus, there's no way my parents would let me do this. I'm their straight-A, Student of the Year daughter. I'm pretty sure this isn't what they have in mind when they say they love seeing me onstage, like at the awards ceremony.

But something inside makes my arm reach out and grab a flyer from the stack on the counter underneath the bulletin board.

A girl can dream, right?

CHAPTER
6

"LILY! CAN YOU GET THE huǒ guō pot, please?" Mom's voice travels from the kitchen to the living room where I'm lounging on our plush brown couch and watching music videos on TV.

I groan from my comfy spot. After my marathon homework session this morning, I'd much rather keep watching music videos.

But duty calls. I peel myself off the couch and head toward our storage space in the condo garage. After rummaging around for a bit, I finally spot the box with our hot pot perched on top of a huge chest.

Ugh.

So.

Heavy.

But if there's the slightest chance I'm going to learn electric guitar this summer, my arms need to get stronger. So I take a deep breath and lug the box out of the garage, up the backyard steps, and to our dining room. Then I set it up in the middle of the table.

When I poke my head into the kitchen, the three adults are chopping up veggies or piling ingredients onto small plates.

"Mom, the huǒ guō is ready. But someone needs to start the gas."

"Okay, no problem. Prepare the rest of the table, will you?" Dad balances a mound of fish balls on a plate.

I pull out chopsticks, soup spoons, wire ladles, and bowls and start to arrange them on the dining table. Right as I put down the last pair of chopsticks, the doorbell rings.

As usual, Vivian and her family are on time for our Saturday night Xiao family dinner.

"Jìn lái, jìn lái!" Ah-ma swings open our front door and ushers Auntie and Uncle in, bending to place slippers at their feet. "Here, here, put these on," Ah-ma fusses in Taiwanese.

"Ma. I know, I know." Auntie's black bob bounces and her smile flashes behind her big tinted glasses. She shoves grocery bags into Ah-ma's hands and exchanges her heels for a pair of red house slippers.

I don't know what it's like at other Taiwanese homes, but when you walk through our front door, you better take off your outdoor shoes as fast as you can. Otherwise, Ah-ma's going to give you a piece of her mind.

"Nǐ hǎo, Auntie, Uncle." I bow a tiny bit and politely address my aunt and uncle. Vivian sticks her tongue out at me as she pulls off her red Chuck Taylors and slips on the blue slippers with bear ears she always wears when she's over.

I laugh softly. She's such a crack-up.

When I showed her the Camp Rock Out flyer earlier today at the library, Vivian's eyes got super big, like Xiǎo Dīng Dāng's. "You mean, we can finally start our band? That would be *so* cool!"

"Maybe?" I whispered back. "But there's no way our parents would go for it."

Vivian shrugged. "We'll never know unless we ask."

"I dunno . . ." I said slowly. I didn't have the heart to tell Vivian that I wasn't actually that sure about Camp Rock Out. What if we asked and our parents said yes? Then I wouldn't have an excuse *not* to go.

"What do American kids usually do over the summer, anyway?" Vivian wondered out loud. "In Taipei, everyone does bǔ xí bān."

I wrinkled my nose. "Ugh, tutoring classes all summer sounds horrible. We're usually with your family, but most Pacific Park kids go to camps. There are camps for sports or Girl Scouts or nature ones, like where you go to the mountains and sleep in log cabins."

Vivian's eyebrows shot up. "Wow, how fun! That's pretty different from what we do in Taipei."

Then she nudged my shoulder. "And hey, studying isn't the most fun thing in the world to do over the summer, but it can help give you a head start. I have to admit that the idea of me spending more time working on my English isn't the worst idea."

"Come on, you're doing just fine," I scoffed. "And there's no way I'm going to do bǔ xí bān. I'm still top of my class!" Honestly, Vivian can be such a worrywart sometimes.

"Fine, fine," she mumbled back. "Maybe let's just see if our parents would be open to the idea of us going to camp at all. You know, start off slow."

I nodded. "That makes sense. If they are, we can bring up the rock part of it later."

Plus, this approach would buy me some time to figure out if going to Camp Rock Out was something I really wanted to do. It still seemed like a super scary idea.

We agreed to test the waters at dinner—and now here we are.

I follow Vivian down the hallway to our dining room, where a sea of plates with cabbage, tofu cubes, mushrooms, chunks of fish, and thin slices of raw meat surround a bubbling pot of soup.

We take our usual seats. For the first few minutes, it's quiet as we each make our own dipping sauces. My favorite mix is with soy sauce, sesame paste, garlic, green onion, a raw egg, and three heaping spoonfuls of shā chá jiàng. Nothing beats the spicy, salty, oily sauce that comes from a silver can with a cartoon bull on it.

We start putting morsels of food into the soup. It only takes a few minutes for the hot pot to cook whatever we put inside, and we scoop up the pieces we want with individual wire ladles or pluck them out with chopsticks.

"Hey, sió-tī, how's your job going?" Auntie asks my dad in Taiwanese as she snags a fish ball. "I hear from Ma that you're up for a promotion soon."

"Yes, there's an open manager position." Dad puts a thin piece of pink lamb into the boiling soup. "If I get it, it'd mean more money for us as a family, and the chance to manage a small team of engineers and testers."

Mom chimes in, grinning at Dad proudly. "He'd also be the first Taiwanese manager at the company. Maybe we could even buy our very own house soon."

Dad shakes his head. "It's not a sure thing, though. My boss, Mr. Williams, doesn't seem too happy with me."

"Oh? Why is that?" Auntie asks. She blows on a chunk of steaming hot tofu.

"Seems that his boss is putting a lot of pressure on him to get our connection speeds up. I talked to Mr. Williams today about my idea, but he doesn't think it will work. I wonder if I should talk directly to his boss about giving it a try."

My ears perk up at what Dad just said. Did my super nice, predictable father suggest that he might do something his boss doesn't want him to?

Ah-ma puts a piece of pork in his bowl. "No, no," she says, shaking her head. "You have to be careful. If Mr. Williams hears you went over his head, he won't be happy. Don't make any trouble."

There she goes again, with another one of her Ah-ma-isms. In my opinion, it's actually pretty cool that my super predictable dad is thinking about stepping up for his idea.

But I don't dare contradict my grandma. She demands respect, and her granddaughter voicing a different opinion isn't it.

"Wait, your idea is what's better for the company, isn't it? It'll show leadership on your part, Steven." Auntie pushes.

Apparently, *she* dares.

"No. Keep your head down, son. Haven't you kids learned anything about what happens if you stand up to people more powerful than you?" Ah-ma says in a sharp tone.

The adults quiet down right away, and for a few seconds, the only sounds are of the bubbling soup.

Whoa. What happened? Vivian and I exchange confused looks.

Mom clears her throat. "So how's school going, kids?" She finds a bright orange shrimp in the pot and places it on my plate.

Good call, Mom. How Vivian and I are doing in school is always a good fallback topic with this crowd.

I pick up the steaming shrimp with my fingers and blow at it. When we were kids, Vivian showed me that the best part of boiled shrimp is the head, which you pull off so you can suck in the yummy saltiness of it.

"School's fine. Nothing special," I say.

"Aren't progress reports coming soon?" she asks.

"Yeah, they should be coming in a few weeks."

"I assume there won't be any surprises?" Mom tosses me a look, eyebrows raised.

I know what Mom actually means: *There better not be any.* Luckily, she has nothing to worry about. Lily Xiao, Sixth Grade Student of the Year, aka class robot, will deliver as programmed.

"Everything should be fine, Mom," I assure her. "I've gotten all As so far this semester."

"And you, Vivian?" Auntie asks, putting her chopsticks down. "I hope to see better grades from you."

Vivian swallows whatever was in her mouth, and her leg jiggles under the table. "I'm trying, Ma," she mutters.

"Keep going," Uncle chimes in. "I know it's not easy. But we can't afford a private English tutor right now."

"It's okay, Lily is helping," Ah-ma asserts.

"That's right!" I flash Vivian a big smile. "You've got me."

"I forgot, when does the school year end here, again?" Auntie asks.

"Summer starts in June." Dad drops some mushrooms into the pot.

At the mention of summer, my ears perk up again. This could be the right moment to test the waters for Camp Rock Out.

"June's only a few months away. Maybe we can start talking about what Vivian and I can do this summer," I say, blinking innocently and trying to keep my voice level.

Auntie crinkles her nose. "What to do? Wouldn't you two go to bǔ xí bān?"

"I think kids here usually choose activities they like and sign up for summer camps," Dad says. "Lily's never gone because we're always in Taiwan."

"Right." I nod. "Maybe Vivian and I can do something fun for our first summer together in Pacific Park."

"Like what?" Uncle slurps up a long noodle.

Mom shrugs. "This is a part of American culture that we don't know much about. If we didn't go back to Taipei every summer, we'd probably have Lily in some kind of tutoring program, too."

Ugh. The only thing Mom ever wants me to do is study. But Camp Rock Out could be my chance to do something different.

Although there's a small part of me that hopes my parents will just say no to the idea of summer camps. That way, I won't have to gather up the courage to actually sign up for Camp Rock Out and that end-of-camp performance!

But something deep inside tells me to keep going.

"Some kids do soccer or art or science camps. There are music camps, too," I say casually.

"Music? Like to play in an orchestra? Or an all-American marching band?" Uncle wipes his mouth with a napkin and pretends to blow a trumpet.

"Yes, things like that. It could be fun to learn something new," I say.

"What's the point of learning music at this stage of your studies, though, Lily? It's probably too late to make anything of it. We should have gotten you started much earlier if this is something you were interested in," Mom says.

"Do I have to do it to help with my future? Couldn't I

learn something new simply because I'm curious about it?" I try to push back.

Mom clicks her tongue. "It feels like you could do something more useful with that time. Plus, it costs money."

I bite my lip. The more she protests, the more I want to fight. Can't I ever do anything for me, just for kicks? Even if it's not learning how to play grunge rock.

"Maybe Vivian and I can do some research first to see what's out there," I suggest.

Auntie furrows her eyebrows. "I don't know. I'd prefer Vivian to keep working on her English, especially if her grades continue as they are."

My heart sinks. I don't want to go to Camp Rock Out by myself. In fact, I don't want to go to any camp by myself. I'd be surrounded by all sorts of new kids without my bubbly cousin by my side. Just thinking about the possibility makes my palms sweat.

And we've spent *every* summer together since we were four. I don't want that to change, especially now that we live in the same city.

I glance at Vivian, who's staring at her bowl with a worried look on her face.

If Auntie is anything like Mom, Vivian's probably doing fine. An A- instead of an A, maybe even a B+ at worst. My mom always used to tell me how well Vivian did in Taipei, probably to motivate me or something.

"We don't need to decide right now," I interject. "I'll keep helping Vivian with her schoolwork. In the meantime, I'll ask around to see what camps might be good for us."

"Okay, Lily. And keep those grades up. That's the most important thing. I don't want any distractions," Mom says.

I nod and do my best to hold back an eye roll.

The adults turn their attention back to fishing out food from the hot pot, and Auntie starts to talk about the fairness of the upcoming city elections here in Pacific Park.

Well, it wasn't a no to Camp Rock Out. But it wasn't a yes, either. Although I'm not sure which one I was hoping to hear.

I stare at the enoki mushrooms sinking in my bowl and concentrate on chewing. Even though my mind's not made up yet about Camp Rock Out, sometimes I wish my parents would just say yes, sure, go ahead, Lily, explore the things that you think look interesting. For fun.

Vivian nudges my shoulder. My face must show how I'm feeling because she flashes me a sympathetic smile, even though *she* was the one getting the brunt of the "you must do well in school" discussion.

"Don't worry about Camp Rock Out, or whatever we end up doing," she whispers. "What matters is that we'll do it together."

She fishes another shrimp out of the hot pot and puts it in my bowl.

I smile at her. She's right. Camp Rock Out or no, bǔ xí bān or not, what matters is that we're together this summer.

Like we are every year.

CHAPTER
7

IT'S MONDAY MORNING, AND I get to my first-period social studies class right as the bell rings. Yoona Kim, my tablemate, is already there, sketching what looks like a manga comic and tapping her foot to what sounds like a mix of rap and rock music blasting from her headphones. Her long, wavy hair frames her face and blue glasses, and she's got a sleeveless denim vest over a neon-purple shirt.

I pull back my chair and motion at Yoona to take her headphones off.

She does, a confused look on her face.

"The bell already rang." I point at the clock on the wall. "You're going to get in trouble with Ms. King again if she catches you listening to music in class." I glance up at the front of the classroom, where Ms. King is getting up from her desk, her wavy brown hair pinned to one side and her long, flowery dress swishing behind her.

"Oh, right. Thanks." Yoona tucks her Walkman into her backpack. "I was listening to this Korean music group I discovered a few days ago, Seo Taiji and Boys."

"That was Korean music?" I'm no expert, but if Korean music is anything like Taiwanese music, it's mostly folky, traditional ballads about patriotism and duty.

"Yes! But they're super different from the usual stuff. That's why I like them."

I smile. "That's awesome. It's always fun to find new music."

"What about you? Still into grunge?"

"Always and forever!" I laugh.

Ms. King claps her hands, and the class simmers down.

"Happy Monday, class. Today, we're going to kick off a unit on the women's suffrage movement. The project for this theme will be done in groups, each with a different topic to give a presentation on."

Ugh. Group projects are the worst. Somehow the other kids expect me to do most of the work because they assume I can do it the best. Group projects are when my robotness is an advantage for everyone but me.

Yoona groans softly.

"Here we go," she mumbles. "More work for me."

I chuckle. She gets it, too.

Ms. King reads off the names of our assigned group members, and I'm in one with Sabrina Morgan, Rebecca Conway, and Logan Ryan.

I recognize Sabrina's name from our old elementary school, but she started going to a different one after she moved neighborhoods in the fourth grade. Rebecca and I are in the same algebra class, and I have third period gym with Logan. Last week, he walked the timed mile instead of running it and got Coach Heilman so angry that he made us all sit and watch Logan finish the final lap instead of free play.

Logan ignored our dirty looks and laughed as he walked over the finish line with a time of twenty-four minutes and thirty-two seconds.

Double ugh that I have to be in a group with him.

"Please get up and find your teammates," Ms. King instructs. "I'll pass out the assignments, and you can spend some time in class deciding how to approach your project."

Yoona heads straight for the back of the classroom, and I spot Logan's bright red hair by the cabinets in the corner.

Logan snickers as he sees me approaching. He leans back in his chair and puts his arms over his head. "Oh, great! It's our Student of the Year. This project will be a breeze."

To some kids at Pacific Park Middle, I'm just one of the smart kids.

Rebecca waves at me, while Sabrina runs her fingers through her short brown hair. "I'm Sabrina," she says. "You're new here, right?"

"No, I'm not new." I stare at her with surprise. She doesn't recognize me from Oak Elementary?

"You're not?" Sabrina looks confused.

And then to other kids, I'm the girl who no one sees.

"Nah, it's the other one who's new, the one who doesn't speak English," Logan says. "Those two are always ching chonging together."

My cheeks get hot. "We don't ching chong. We speak in Chinese."

"Whatever." Logan rolls his eyes. "Same difference."

I grit my teeth. I look around for Ms. King because someone needs to tell her what a jerk this guy is.

But then I hear echoes of Ah-ma's voice. *Keep your head down. Don't cause trouble.*

I bite my lip instead. I don't want to cause a scene.

It doesn't matter, anyway, because Ms. King's at our table handing out our assignment. "I'd like your group to research the techniques and tactics that the women of the suffrage movement used to advocate for the right to vote. Prepare a fifteen-minute presentation for next week. The information you'll need is in chapter twenty-one, although I encourage you to use other sources, too."

I nod obediently while Logan puts his feet up on a nearby chair. Once she's out of earshot, Logan groans. "What a boring topic."

I actually think it's kind of cool to learn about what women did to fight for the right to vote. I don't say anything, though, and reach into my backpack for my American history textbook. What's the point? Nothing the class robot can say is going to change anyone's mind about anything. Especially someone like Logan.

As anger bubbles inside my body with no place to go, Camp Rock Out is feeling more and more like a good idea.

An intense, Eddie-like growl sure could hit the spot right now.

When I get home from school, Ah-ma asks me if I can go to the supermarket with her to pick up some stuff for dinner tonight. She says she needs my help carrying the bags home.

The truth is, she could outlift me because of how much tài jí she does, no problem. But Ah-ma gets nervous leaving the house on her own. Her English isn't great, and she worries she'll get lost.

I have to wait a half hour before we can go, though. Ah-ma always insists on looking just right whenever she walks out our front door, so it takes at least two wardrobe changes and an unpredictable amount of time to get her hair to puff up perfectly.

When she's finally ready, I can't deny that she looks pretty fierce in her flowery bomber jacket, purple slacks, and huge tortoiseshell sunglasses. And her rooster updo, of course.

The supermarket is in the same plaza as Power Records, and we have to walk by the record store first. As we get close, I notice two boys sitting at the curb with skateboards at their feet. One's got a bright red beanie on, with straight blond hair smooshed around the edges, and the green cap of the other boy is on backward. Loud music blares from a pair of shared earphones.

It's Ketchup Boy and Marcos Alvarez.

Ugh. I don't want to see *them* again.

I duck my head down and try to look invisible as Ah-ma and I approach. But as we walk by, Marcos pulls out his earbud. "Hey, it's you. Hold up a sec."

I stop in my tracks. What does *he* want?

"Tsa-bóo-sun, you talk to your friend, and I'll meet you inside, okay?" Ah-ma squeezes my arm and continues to shuffle toward the supermarket.

"Oh, no, it's okay . . ." I start to say. But for some

reason, Ah-ma decides to move at warp speed at this terribly inconvenient moment, and before I can blink twice, she's already halfway to her destination.

Well, there goes my excuse to avoid these two boys.

Meanwhile, Ketchup Boy glances up at me, takes the earbud from Marcos, and puts it in his other ear. He keeps bobbing his head to whatever music he's listening to, completely ignoring me.

Whew. One less skater boy to deal with.

"Uh, what?" I turn toward Marcos and nervously tug at the tails of my flannel button-down. There's probably a rude or weird comment coming.

"You're Lily, right?" Marcos says. "Didn't we go to Oak Elementary together?"

Whoa, he remembers? I try to stay cool and nod silently in response.

"So you're into grunge, huh? Me too. I got a new album that's pretty cool. Wanna hear it?"

As my insides whirl in a desperate attempt to conjure up the nerve to say yes, I notice how Marcos's lashes curl up in an almost-perfect circle, like the wisps of chocolate-brown hair that have escaped from beneath his baseball hat.

But then Ketchup Boy stretches his legs out straight, clearly bored, and the image of him laughing at Keiko yesterday flashes into my brain. Marcos is friends with this jerk, which means they must think alike. Does

Marcos want to show me new music, or is he setting me up for some awful joke about being a weird Asian chick who likes grunge?

It's got to be the last thing. Why else would he talk to someone like me?

"Uh, no, it's okay," I mumble. I quickly turn away and run toward the supermarket.

As the glass doors of the market slide open, I groan in my head.

I'm so *not* grunge. Eddie Vedder would have handled that in a much cooler "who cares" way.

But I don't have an ounce of Eddie-level energy in me. Yet.

Now that I'm at the market, I scan the crowd that's mingling around the entrance for Ah-ma. I spot her bright purple bomber jacket right as she reaches for the last shopping cart.

Suddenly, a man in a business suit dashes forward, grabs it from under her hands, and starts wheeling it away.

"Hey! What are you doing?" I shout. I leap to Ah-ma's side and pull her close.

He looks over his shoulder, contempt all over his face. "I was faster. You snooze, you lose."

"But . . ." I splutter. "She was reaching for it. And she needs it more than you do!"

He waves us off. "Hey, if you don't like how we do

things here, you two can go back to where you came from."

What?! My face flushes red. I *am* where I came from!

Ah-ma's hand suddenly comes down hard on my arm, tight as a vise. She waves at the man to take the cart, bowing slightly. "For you, for you . . ."

Then she drags me out of sight. "Zǒu, zǒu. Don't cause any trouble, Lily. It's okay. I don't need it. We'll find another one."

"Ah-ma! What he said was totally racist! We can't let him get away with it!" I may be a chicken when someone messes with me, but it's another thing to mess with my grandma. I try to pull my way back so I can get Ah-ma what she deserves.

"Stop. It's fine," Ah-ma repeats. "It's not our place to fight with people like that. Calm yourself, please."

A store employee appears, pulling a train of shopping carts behind her. Ah-ma points. "Tsa-bóo-sun, go get me a cart now. Problem solved."

I grit my teeth and stomp my way over to the carts. I sulk as Ah-ma calmly walks down the aisles, inspecting products and dropping them into the cart like nothing happened.

But I'm still fuming.

I finally had a chance to speak up and let someone have it, rocker-style. But I can't believe Ah-ma stopped me. She's like Jekyll and Hyde. When she's with our family, she's this strong, opinionated woman who doesn't let us get away with anything. But in front of other people, especially people who look kinda "official," she crumbles like a flaky egg tart. She never wants to stand up to anyone, even when they blatantly offend her like that horrible man did.

She won't even let *me* stand up for her.

As the fire in my belly burns, Ah-ma finishes her shopping, and we head back home. My feet fall heavy against the pavement, and I hug the grocery bag tightly to my chest, like that'll slow down its angry pounding.

Then, as we walk by the doors of Power Records, the front curb now empty, I recognize Eddie Vedder's signature growl echoing from the store speakers. Even from outside, I can hear the passion and anger of the whole band as their music spills into the Pacific Park air.

My eyes linger on the Pearl Jam poster on the shop window. Together, these guys make up the coolest grunge band in the world . . . and they look so normal. No one could guess how passionate and deep and angry they really are.

And how loud they can be.

I look like a normal nice girl, too. That's why people like Logan and this horrible man walk all over me. And Ah-ma, too, although I think she looks pretty fierce. But to the outside world, apparently she looks like a small, meek old Asian woman.

My dad's also a bit of a chicken. He's got a great idea but is too afraid to bring it to his boss's boss.

The entire Xiao family could use a lesson on how to be more grunge.

But I'm the only one with a chance to learn a thing or two about how to speak up and make people pay attention. If I go to Camp Rock Out, they'll teach me how to be bolder. The music, the vibes, the energy—all of it. Then I can be loud and angry in front of people like that awful man, Ketchup Boy, Marcos, or Logan, even if someone tries to stop me.

Maybe some of that grit will rub off on my family, too. If they see me up onstage, rocking out with so much power, maybe they'll see that you can speak up, too . . . and not get in trouble.

As I stand in front of Power Records, with the heavy riffs of Pearl Jam washing over me, I make a decision.

I need to go to Camp Rock Out. I need to learn how to be grunge.

Not only for me, though. For my family, too.

Robot: prepare for transformation sequence.

CHAPTER
8

THE NEXT DAY, I'M SITTING at one of the stone benches in our usual lunch spot, jiggling my leg nervously as I wait for Vivian. It's already ten minutes into lunch period, and I need her so we can figure out how to get our parents to sign us up for Camp Rock Out.

I discovered this place the second week of school when I glanced out the library window at recess and noticed how this spot was always empty. It was nicer to be outside than indoors, so I'd hang out here at lunch by myself, studying or reading the manga I'd brought back from Taipei. After Vivian moved to Pacific Park in October, this was the perfect spot where we could chatter away in Chinese without anyone judging us.

Like Logan did.

Once I'm done with Camp Rock Out, I'm going to give that jerk a piece of my mind.

Vivian rushes into the courtyard and plops her backpack down onto one of the stone benches. "I'm so sorry you had to wait for me! I couldn't finish my class assignment, so the teacher held me back."

"It's okay." I hand her the biàn dang Ah-ma made for her, along with a pair of chopsticks.

Vivian opens the lid and takes a sniff. "Oh, it's lǔ ròu fàn with bok choy today!"

When I got up this morning, I was still annoyed at Ah-ma for not giving me a chance to defend her at the market. But when I saw her stirring the bubbling pot of braised fatty pork, which I know takes hours to cook, my anger melted away.

Ah-ma will never say she's sorry—that word isn't in her vocabulary. But I know her making my favorite lunch is her way of saying, "I know what you tried to do. And I appreciate it."

Vivian shovels rice into her mouth. "So what's new, biǎo jiě?"

"Well, yesterday pretty much sucked." I tell her what happened at the supermarket through a mouthful of bok choy.

"Oh no," she breathes out. "I can't believe that man said such awful things."

"I know, it was horrible. I tried to defend Ah-ma, but she wouldn't let me."

Vivian shrugs. "Yeah, that's Ah-ma for you. When we were at a restaurant the other day, she wouldn't let Dad send back the pasta they gave her, even though they got her order wrong."

"We were both total chickens yesterday." I hang my head in embarrassment. "So I've been thinking . . ."

I pause.

Do I really think I can make music like Eddie Vedder? And be as grunge as he is?

Vivian looks at me with her big eyes blinking under her bangs, patiently waiting. Seeing her reminds me of how brave she's been—moving to a new country, going to a new school, learning a whole new language . . .

If my biǎo mèi can do all that, I can get up onstage and play rock music.

I grit my teeth. "I want to go to Camp Rock Out. I want to learn how to be more grunge, so I don't lose my voice like that again."

Vivian's chopsticks stop in midair. "Wait, I thought you wanted to go. Isn't that why we asked about summer camps at dinner the other night?"

"Well," I confess sheepishly, "to be honest, I wasn't so sure. There's the performance . . ."

"Psh." Vivian rolls her eyes. "It's like those piano

recitals I had to do back in Taipei. You practice enough, and the rhythm becomes automatic."

I think back to my Student of the Year speech. That was part of the problem—it became automatic. How do I get up onstage and project something besides total awkwardness?

"As long as you're there with me, biǎo mèi, I think I'll be able to do it. We're doing the camp together, right?" I pull at her sleeve.

Vivian swallows whatever was in her mouth. "You heard my mom and dad—they want me to do English bǔ xí bān this summer."

"You've been studying so hard all year. You think they'll make you go?"

Vivian looks down at her half-eaten lunch. "It might not be that bad of an idea for me to get some extra tutoring this summer. School's been so tough."

I blow out an exasperated sigh. "Come on, Vivian! You have to relax. Your English is fine."

"Yeah, maybe." She doesn't meet my gaze, though, and picks at her rice with her chopsticks instead.

I'm sure my future drummer is worried about nothing. The kind of homework we have to do here must be a breeze compared to what she had to do in Taipei.

But she still seems nervous. Maybe this is a chance for me to do the big cousin thing and help her out.

"Have you thought about asking your teachers for some extra tutoring?" I ask.

Vivian looks up at me, a strange look on her face. "I dunno . . . is that a thing? In Taipei, if you need extra time with a teacher or a tutor, you pay for it."

I shrug. "I don't know. But schools are where you're supposed to learn. If you're not keeping up, I'm sure the school will do something if you ask for it."

"Oh, I couldn't do that. What if they don't understand my English? And my parents won't ask. They aren't that comfortable talking to teachers," Vivian admits. "As you know, their English isn't that much better than mine."

Now that I think about it, I don't think Mom and Dad have ever really talked to my teachers, either. Their English is fine, so that's not what stops them. But I remember how much Mom and Dad stressed out the first time they had a parent-teacher conference when I was in the first grade. Dad put on the red tie he only wears at Lunar New Year, and Mom wore her fancy black heels. They even showed up a whole hour early.

I guess meeting with your kid's teacher can be a bit nerve-racking, no matter what language you speak.

"What class do you need the most help on?" I ask.

"English lit," Vivian admits. "I'm behind on the reading. There are so many characters and plot twists in *The Westing Game* that I get confused. If I can understand the story, I think I'd be able to write a decent essay."

"I've finished the book. Maybe I can tell you what happens," I offer.

"No, no, that'd be cheating. I should read it myself."

I have to admire her honesty. "Yeah, I get it. If your parents won't ask, maybe I should. I can ask Mr. Silvers if he can help somehow after class today."

Vivian furrows her eyebrows. "Are you sure that's allowed? I dunno, biǎo jiě."

"Come on!" I plead. "You heard our parents at dinner. For us to go to any camp this summer, they're going to want to see good progress grades from us. You do want to go to Camp Rock Out, don't you?"

Vivian crinkles up her nose. "I don't know. I mean, I do . . . but what about my schoolwork? It feels like it's one step forward, two steps back. I just . . . I just don't know if I can do it on my own. Maybe you should go to the camp while I do English bǔ xí bān."

Oh no. Going to Camp Rock Out without my bubbly cousin by my side? Out of the question.

"What if I got you help now? Then you wouldn't need bǔ xí bān this summer," I say, more urgently this time.

Vivian breathes out slowly. "Okay, fine. But only ask Mr. Silvers for now, though."

"Woo-hoo!" I whoop. "You'll see, it's going to be all

right, biǎo mèi. You only need a little boost, that's all. Weren't you in the top of your class at your old middle school?"

"Yeah, I was."

"English lit is just a small bump in the road. Your hard work will pay off, I'm sure it will. You trust your biǎo jiě, right, Vivian?" I insist.

"Yes," she says slowly.

"I got it, biǎo mèi," I reassure her.

But as I munch on Ah-ma's lǔ ròu fàn and listen to Vivian chatter about how it'll be so nice to spend a summer without the hot, muggy stickiness of Taipei, a funny feeling starts to churn inside.

I'm pretty sure my parents won't be thrilled about the idea of me asking a teacher for a favor. Ah-ma, neither. Even a cool teacher like Mr. Silvers probably falls into the category of authority who must not be bothered, questioned, or challenged, like our landlord or the postman with the wet letters.

Or a well-dressed man in a business suit with a shopping cart.

I try to ignore my doubt, though. For Camp Rock Out—and my biǎo mèi—doing one little thing my parents won't approve of will be worth it.

I hope.

CHAPTER
9

AFTER THE END-OF-THE-DAY BELL RINGS, I stuff my things into my backpack and head up to Mr. Silvers's podium at the front of the class. The rest of the class spills out of the classroom, and I wait patiently for Mr. Silvers to finish wiping down the chalkboard.

When he finally turns around, he jumps a bit.

"Ah, Lily, you startled me!" Mr. Silvers sets the erasers down and wipes his chalky hands on his green sweater vest, leaving white handprints on his belly. "What can I do for you?"

Time for me to step up to the mic. "Mr. Silvers, I wanted to ask you about my cousin, Vivian Lin."

"Ah, yes, Vivian's in my first period class." He pushes his glasses up his nose and walks to his desk in the corner. He settles into his chair, leaning back as he puts his arms above his head. It creaks under his weight. "Nice girl—she's trying so hard."

"She's studying a ton," I say. "But she's having a little trouble with *The Westing Game*."

"It's not an easy book for anyone. But I have faith in my students, especially anyone who's related to our Student of the Year."

I smile weakly. It's nice to be appreciated, but also kind of weird that he thinks she'll do well because we happen to be family.

"Um, I wonder if there's a way you can give her some extra help. . . . Maybe work with her after school? I think a real teacher will help her feel better about how she's doing."

Mr. Silvers's face softens. "Oh, Lily, I wish I could. But I don't have the time, nor the teaching credentials, to give ESL learners like Vivian the type of support they need."

I furrow my eyebrows. "ESL? What's that?"

"ESL stands for English as a Second Language. It's how we refer to kids who already read, write, and speak in a different language and are exposed to English later in life. Some districts call it ELL, for English Language Learners."

It's a good sign that there's a shorthand way to talk

about kids like Vivian. It means that she's not the only one.

"If you don't have the teaching credentials, Mr. Silvers, who does?" I ask.

He sighs. "Up until six years ago, every California public school was required to offer special classes taught by trained professionals who focus on teaching the English language to ESL students. We've got a lot of English learners coming from places like Mexico, China, Taiwan, the Philippines, to name a few. Teaching them English in their native languages, which is called bilingual education, helps them learn more easily and faster. That transition of mixing languages is smoother than making them learn everything in English all at once."

"So what happened?" I ask. "Why doesn't Pacific Park Middle offer bilingual education anymore?"

"A few years ago, in 1986 I think, there was a law passed in California called Proposition 63. It made English the official language of our state. Because of that, the federal government stopped giving schools money to pay for bilingual classes. There was no money to train the teachers, either." Mr. Silvers pulls off his glasses and rubs the bridge of his nose, like he's tired. "Slowly, any kind of ESL support went away completely."

I bite my lip, thinking. "Does that mean schools can't do anything at all?"

"Oh, no, they can. But they don't have to," Mr. Silvers

quickly clarifies. "There are a few private schools in the area, like Evergreen Prep, that offer good ESL programs. But their tuition is quite expensive."

Hm, getting Vivian a boost of help is turning out to be more complicated than I thought. "Is there anything *you* can do, Mr. Silvers?"

Mr. Silvers leans forward in his chair. "The truth is, I've talked to Principal Klein a few times about putting ESL students in a special class for some focused attention."

At the mention of Principal Klein, my heart leaps. Our school principal is always going on and on about academic excellence. That's why she started the whole Student of the Year thing, to recognize those of us who are excelling and to use us as examples. She must get why ESL support would help a bunch of her students.

"What did Principal Klein say?"

"She said that Pacific Park Middle doesn't have enough money to pay for classes like that on our own. She'd have to ask the district for the funding."

Bummer. My heart drops back down, and I fiddle with the ends of my flannel shirt. There's got to be something else.

"Could Vivian read an easier book? *The Westing Game* has so many characters that it's not easy to follow the story," I suggest.

"It's required reading in this year's seventh grade curriculum," Mr. Silvers replies.

"What about giving Vivian extra time to finish it? Could she turn in her paper a little later?"

Mr. Silvers thinks for a bit. "Hm, I can do that. Given her circumstances, I'll give her an extra week to turn in her paper. I'll grade hers last, right before I have to turn in mid-quarter progress grades. How's that, Lily?"

An extra week might be enough time for Vivian to finish the reading and get her paper in good shape. So I nod.

But I still don't get why there aren't ESL classes offered at Pacific Park Middle. Isn't it the school's job to give every student a fair chance to learn what they need to? There's got to be money somewhere for that.

I open my mouth to say what I'm thinking. But I hear echoes of Ah-ma in my head again.

Don't cause trouble. Keep your head down.

I decide to be grateful instead. "Thanks, Mr. Silvers. I think an extra week will help."

I turn to leave, but something Mr. Silvers said earlier makes me spin back around. "Mr. Silvers, are there a lot of other ESL kids like Vivian at Pacific Park Middle?"

"Yes, there are." He flips open a notebook on his desk and runs his finger down the page. "Let's see. . . . Yoona Kim asked me for help for Korean students a few months ago. I also see more and more kids from Southeast Asia, like Vietnam or Cambodia, struggle in my class. Our

Spanish-speaking student numbers are increasing a lot, too. California is getting more and more diverse, which is pretty exciting. But with that diversity comes some challenges."

What he's saying doesn't make sense. "But, Mr. Silvers, if so many kids need help, wouldn't that be a big enough reason for Principal Klein to ask the district for more funding?"

"It's complicated, Lily. But why don't you talk to Principal Klein yourself? Maybe she'll do more if it's coming from you." He smiles at me encouragingly. "You're last year's Student of the Year. You've got some influence."

Gulp. It's one thing to talk to Mr. Silvers. But Principal Klein? She's big time. What if I get in trouble for poking around where I shouldn't?

It doesn't seem fair, though, that there are so many kids at Pacific Park Middle who need English help, and the school isn't doing anything for them. The idea of talking to Principal Klein is scary, but maybe Mr. Silvers is right. Maybe being Student of the Year does give me some sway.

My parents would not be cool with me asking the principal for a favor, though.

But I need Camp Rock Out, my brain screams. *So does Vivian. And my whole family.*

"Okay, Mr. Silvers. I'll talk to Principal Klein," I say.

My heart starts to beat faster the second those words leave my mouth.

"Great. She's usually in her office at this time on a Tuesday afternoon, Lily. Good luck, and to Vivian, also. You're a good cousin to be watching out for her like this." Mr. Silvers flashes me a thumbs-up.

As I escape out the door, my insides mix with a flurry of emotions. I'm relieved that I managed to get Vivian some more time to finish the English lit assignment. Hopefully that will be enough to make her feel better about the upcoming progress grades.

But at the same time, it feels like a Band-Aid on a bigger problem, and one that affects more kids at Pacific Park Middle than Vivian.

Even worse, now I have to get in front of the most powerful person at Pacific Park Middle and ask her for something she's already said no to, according to Mr. Silvers.

Camp Rock Out better be worth it.

CHAPTER
10

I'VE DELIVERED ATTENDANCE SHEETS TO the principal's office before, so I know that there are two doors you have to walk through. The first one leads to the general office, where there's a set of cubbies to the right and a long wooden bench to the left. Right in front is the counter where Ms. Jensen, the principal's aide, sits. You have to first check in with her, and after she lets Principal Klein know you're here through the phone intercom, you wait on the bench until Principal Klein calls you into her actual office, which is behind the counter and directly in back.

So after I say goodbye to Mr. Silvers and make my way across campus to the administration building, I push the first door open like it's no big deal. It's the second door that's scary.

But when I step into the waiting room, I stop in my tracks.

Because sitting there on the wooden bench next to the door to Principal's Klein's office is Marcos Alvarez.

What kind of trouble has he gotten into now?

Marcos has his usual baseball cap on, and his sticker-covered skateboard is propped upright against his knee.

"Hey, it's you again." He tilts his chin up in a typical skater-boy greeting. "What are you doing here?"

"Uh, I'm here to talk to Principal Klein about something," I reply shyly, my face starting to flush pink at the memory of me running away from him yesterday at Power Records.

But Marcos just looks back at me through those long eyelashes. Without Ketchup Boy around, he seems less . . . threatening.

"Why are you here?" I manage to ask.

He twirls the wheel on his skateboard, sending it into motion in a smooth, satisfying, neon-green blur. "I'm here to help my aunt and uncle with an appointment they have with Principal Klein. They don't speak English very well, so I'm going to translate for them."

My eyebrows pop up in surprise. He's here to help his family?

"I do that for my cousin sometimes, too," I admit. "She's having some trouble keeping up with reading and writing in English. Our parents won't ask for extra help, so I'm going to ask Principal Klein for it."

Marcos looks at me with a strange expression on his face. "You? You're going to ask the principal for extra help?"

"Yeah." My jerk radar suddenly clicks on. "What's wrong with that?"

He shrugs. "I guess I assumed you wouldn't ask the principal for more than what she's already giving us. You know, Student of the Year and all that."

I stand a smidge taller. "What's that supposed to mean?"

"I mean, you're like every teacher's favorite student. Why challenge the system that's gotten you to where you're at?"

Uh-oh. Marcos has a point. Mr. Silvers thought that me being Student of the Year meant Principal Klein would pay more attention to what I have to say. But what if he's wrong and me questioning why there aren't ESL classes at Pacific Park Middle makes me look ungrateful instead? What if it's worse that the Student of the Year challenges her, instead of supports her decisions?

Doubt begins to creep into my veins. Am I seriously going to ask Principal Klein to change her mind? She already said no to Mr. Silvers when he asked.

Marcos keeps looking at me, like he's expecting me to

say more. But I don't know what to say. If Vivian were here, she'd know what to do.

But she's not.

A few awkward seconds tick by until Marcos reaches into his backpack and pulls out a CD. "By the way, this is the album I was telling you about the other day. I know you said you weren't interested, but I'm telling you, it's pretty sick."

I blush again at the memory of me freaking out and running into the supermarket. The truth is, I'm super curious about what music he's talking about. So I take the CD and read the words on the cover. "Oh, it's the Smashing Pumpkins," I exclaim excitedly. "I've heard of them before."

"You have?" Marcos asks, his head tilted. "I thought they were new on the scene."

"Yeah, they kinda are. But I read about them in a magazine the other day," I reply.

"Their music is so good. A bit different from the Nirvana/Pearl Jam/Soundgarden vibe. You can borrow it if you want," Marcos offers.

"Really?" No one's ever lent me a CD before.

"Yeah, I'm not worried about someone like you messing it up or anything."

Sigh. There it is again—Lily Xiao, perfect little class robot.

But it's a small price to pay for new music. "Okay,

thanks. I'd love to borrow it." I tuck the album safely into my backpack.

"By the way, I don't only listen to grunge music. I play it, too." He grins at me proudly.

"You do?" I don't know anyone in a real rock band besides Keiko.

Although now that I think about it, it makes sense that Marcos is in a rock band. He fits the grunge look and vibe perfectly: boys with long hair and baseball caps or beanies, a "who cares" attitude, T-shirts, baggy jeans, and skateboards.

But Keiko's in a rock band, too, and she's just as grunge as Marcos.

What exactly does it take to be grunge, anyway?

I fiddle with the zipper on my backpack. "How did you learn to play?"

Marcos shrugs and starts to spin the wheels of his skateboard again. "My older brother's in college and he taught me. He lets me use his stuff all the time. Plus, I go to this camp every summer."

"Camp Rock Out?" I blurt out.

"Yeah." He looks at me, his right eyebrow arched. "You know it?"

I nod. "My cousin and I want to go this summer."

"Whoa, girls like you two going to Camp Rock Out? That'd be a first." He laughs.

Something hot in my chest rises to the surface.

"What's that supposed to mean?" My voice comes out louder than I expected it to.

"No girls ever come to Camp Rock Out. And no one who . . . you know . . . looks like you. Have you ever gotten loud and angry? I have to say, I can't picture it."

At his words, my face flashes red. Is he making fun of the idea of Asian girls like me and Vivian going to Camp Rock Out? What matters is that we love the music. That's enough for us to belong there. . . .

Isn't it?

And what's this about us not being able to get loud and angry? Of course we can get that way! I would have exploded if Ah-ma didn't stop me at the supermarket.

In fact, I feel it flare up now. It's time to say something and put this guy in his place.

Suddenly, the door to the principal's office swings open, and Principal Klein appears in the doorway, tapping her foot impatiently.

And just like that, the flame inside me, ready to fight Marcos Alvarez, completely dies out, like a bucket of water has been dumped over my head. Clearly, my family's caution around authority figures has totally rubbed off on me, because seeing the ultimate authority at Pacific Park Middle stops me cold.

I mean, she calls *all* the shots around here.

Plus, Principal Klein is built tall and sturdy, with

her brownish-gray hair piled up high on her head, like Ah-ma's, which makes her look even bigger. Her usual outfit of stiff, button-up gray or tan blouses and pencil skirts that hit at the knee makes her look all business, and her heels make a distinct *clip-clop* sound as she walks around the school, visiting classrooms and tending to . . . whatever it is principals do all day.

"Marcos," Principal Klein says sternly, arms crossed. "What are you doing here? Did you get in trouble again today?"

"No, ma'am," he responds politely, although I can see his cheeks redden slightly under his tan skin.

Meanwhile, I'm a bit taken aback by how quickly Principal Klein assumed Marcos was here for doing something bad. Although, I thought the exact same thing when I first saw him.

"I'm here to help my aunt and uncle with the meeting they have with you this afternoon. Their son, Carlos Garcia, is my cousin."

"Ah, I didn't realize they were your family. And they're running late," she says, pointing at her watch with a long finger.

"They should be here any minute, ma'am." Marcos stands up, hoisting his backpack up onto his shoulders. "Sometimes the buses get delayed."

"Lily Xiao!" Principal Klein suddenly exclaims,

noticing me for the first time. "To what do I owe the pleasure? How's our Student of the Year doing?"

I squirm under her sharp gaze and my palms get clammy. But I push myself to answer. "I'd like to talk to you about my cousin, too," I say with all the confidence I can muster.

"I'm intrigued." Principal Klein arches her left eyebrow. "This meeting shouldn't take long. Can you wait a bit?"

I nod.

The waiting room door suddenly creaks open, and a woman with long dark hair peers inside. She's got Marcos's soft eyelashes, although her hair is much curlier and cascades down her back in waves. When she spots Marcos, a big smile breaks across her face.

"¡Ya llegamos!" She turns around and calls out into the hallway. "Está aquí."

A man in a black fleece jacket and worn jeans appears behind her. They shuffle in hesitantly.

"Hola, tíos." Marcos beckons them in. "Principal Klein, this is my aunt and uncle, Graciela and Juve Garcia. They're here to talk to you about how Carlos is doing in school."

The two of them bow slightly and hunch their bodies in a way that strikes me as familiar. Where have I seen this energy before?

It hits me. Ah-ma had the same body language with

that awful man at the supermarket. Like she was bow-ing down to someone superior to her.

"Thank you for coming. Let's go inside so we can talk." Principal Klein ushers them into her office.

Marcos speaks to his aunt and uncle in Spanish, then the four of them head into the principal's office.

As I watch them leave, my head whirls. Laughing at the idea of me and Vivian going to Camp Rock Out makes Marcos a total jerk. But he's also a protector of his family, like I am with Ah-ma and Vivian.

Plus, he lent me his Smashing Pumpkins album.

Maybe skater boys have more than one side to them, too.

Like class robots do.

Ten minutes later, Principal Klein's door opens up again. Marcos's aunt and uncle shuffle out, clutching white papers to their chests. Marcos trudges behind them, scowling.

I turn off the music I'd been listening to. "Are you okay, Marcos?" I whisper.

"This school is so unfair," he mutters. "Principal Klein says my cousin isn't doing well enough in class because of his English. But at the same time, she's not going to do anything to help him get better," Marcos growls. "Ven-gan, vamos a casa." He leads his aunt and uncle out of the office, and the door bangs shut behind them.

"Lily, come on in. I'm ready for you now," Principal Klein calls out from her office.

Now it's my turn.

Uh-oh. If Marcos struck out, that means I'm going to strike out, too. There's no way she's going to say yes to me if she's already said no to Marcos and his family.

Mr. Silvers has tried asking her for more ESL help, too. If other people couldn't change Principal Klein's mind, how am I going to?

Robot: abort mission.

CHAPTER
11

WHEN I GET HOME, AH-MA'S already sitting at the dining room table. Instead of preparing mung beans today, though, she's kneading a white lump of dough on a big wooden board. On the table is a bowl with a pair of chopsticks resting on its rim, a baking sheet covered in aluminum foil, and a small cup of water.

"Ah-ma, wǒ dào jiā le." I drop my backpack on the floor and join her.

"Welcome home," Ah-ma grunts in Taiwanese as she leans into the dough. "Guess what I'm making?"

I take a closer look at what she's kneading, which is stickier and starchier than the dough we use for wrapping soup dumplings or potstickers. Inside the silver bowl are ground pork, mushrooms, and bamboo shoots, and I spot a bottle of sweet chili sauce on the table.

"Are you making bah-oân?" I ask.

"Yes!" She laughs, wiping her brow with the back of her hand. "Your mom's favorite!"

Whenever we go to night markets in Taipei, Mom's always on the lookout for these sticky meatball dumplings. Ah-ma knows how to make them with sweet potato starch and rice flour from the Chinese market. Plus, she has a special recipe to get the bah-oân dough thicker and kneadable, rather than its more traditional gooeyness that you have to spoon into individual bowls for each dumpling. Ah-ma's way is much easier—and faster.

"What have you been up to, tsa-bóo-sun?" Ah-ma asks. "You're a bit later coming home from school than usual."

Uh-oh. There's no way Ah-ma would be cool with the fact that I went to Principal Klein to ask for ESL classes for Vivian.

Not that I actually went through with it. After Marcos's family left and Principal Klein invited me into her office, I got up from the bench and, thinking fast, told her that I was there to say thanks again for the Student of the Year award she gave me last year.

"Of course, Lily!" She beamed. "You're a perfect example of what can happen when someone works hard to achieve excellence. Especially as someone from another country."

Wait, I was born here, I wanted to respond.

But I bit my tongue instead and hightailed it out of there. I'd already chickened out of asking for ESL classes. I didn't have the guts to correct Principal Klein's mistake, either.

And I definitely don't have the guts to tell my authority-fearing grandmother that I almost went up to the most powerful person at Pacific Park Middle to ask for a favor.

"Uh, I was working on that group project I told you about yesterday," I lie.

Ah-ma flips the dough over and keeps working it. "That's good. What's the project about again? I know very little about American history."

I'd done my reading during class, as instructed, so luckily I had enough to make my lie believable. "It's about the women's suffrage movement, which was when women wanted the right to vote and protested the US government to get it. They eventually won, and women's right to vote became the Nineteenth Amendment."

"That's it? Women asked and the government just gave them what they wanted?" Ah-ma tsks. "How nice to be American."

"It wasn't as easy as that." I pick up the chopsticks and give the stuffing a good mix. "The suffragettes had to fight pretty hard for it, with petitions and marches and other smart moves. And not all American women got to vote. It was only white women at first. African Americans, Latinas, even Asian Americans like us weren't allowed to vote until much later. Asians couldn't even become citizens until the 1950s."

As I tell Ah-ma the story, my blood starts to boil. Back then, if you were a girl, things were pretty tough. If on top of that, you weren't white, life was even more unfair.

Thank goodness things are different now. Even someone like me, born in the US from a Taiwanese family, can vote when I'm old enough.

"Humph," Ah-ma grumbles. "Speaking up like that sounds awfully risky to me."

I glance at Ah-ma, who avoids my eyes as she presses the dough a few more times. What is it about her and the government?

Ah-ma rolls the dough into a thick log and picks up her cleaver. "Go wash your hands, Lily, and help me," she says.

What I really want to do is go to my room and recover from today's nerve-racking afternoon.

But Ah-ma's looking at me so expectantly that I head into the kitchen like the obedient granddaughter she's trained me to be instead.

I can't fail her, even in her bah-oân-making expectations.

When I join Ah-ma back at the dining table, she's already cut the dough into medium-sized chunks. We each take a piece and press it onto the table to make a flat disk. Next up is scooping and putting filling on them. Then I cup the bah-oân in one hand and pinch it closed as tightly as I can with the other.

"Tell me more about your day, tsa-bóo-sun," Ah-ma says.

I hesitate. The only thing that pops into my head that might be safe enough to share is my confusing conversation with Marcos.

But thinking about what he said about girls like me and Vivian going to Camp Rock Out makes the seed of doubt he planted take firmer root. Maybe us going to a rock-and-roll camp *is* a bad idea.

I guess I hesitated too long before responding, because Ah-ma stops mid-scoop and stares at me, her right eyebrow arched high. "Lily? What's going on?"

I have to give her something. "Remember when we were talking about summer camps the other night with Auntie and Uncle?"

Ah-ma nods.

"I found one that Vivian and I want to go to. It'd teach us how to play that music we like."

"Ah yes. They do this in the videos I see you watching

on the television set." She wiggles her head up and down, her updo jiggling.

I giggle at Ah-ma headbanging. "Yes, exactly."

Marcos's laugh echoes in my brain. "But I don't think we should do it. Maybe this type of music is better for me to listen to, not to play. I mean, can you imagine someone like me onstage with a guitar, rocking out like they do? I couldn't. It'd look . . . ridiculous." I shake my head at the image.

Ah-ma puts down the bun in her hand and looks at me thoughtfully. "You want to play the guitar?"

I avoid her eyes and shrug my shoulders.

She reaches out and tilts my chin toward her. "Did you know that your ah-gong played the guitar?"

I stare at Ah-ma in surprise. "He did?"

Ah-ma barely ever talks about my grandfather. All I know is that he died when my dad was a baby, although I don't know how.

I never ask Ah-ma about him, either. Every time I bring him up, Ah-ma gets quiet, and Dad changes the subject superfast, like he doesn't want to give the memory of his father the chance to come up.

The fact that Ah-ma's brought him up on her own feels like a special gift.

Ah-ma smiles. "Yes, one of his most treasured possessions was an acoustic guitar that a US soldier gave to him when Ah-gong was working as a translator for the American army after we got married. He'd play it every day. He'd even play a few tunes to your dad when I was pregnant." She stares into the distance with a sad expression on her face.

My heart softens at the image of my grandfather sitting at Ah-ma's feet and strumming sweet lullabies to her big belly. "Why are you telling me this?" I ask softly.

"I used to tease him that he looked ridiculous with a guitar in his hand, like a fake American cowboy. But he loved playing anyway. When I look back, I'm glad he kept going. It made him happy." Ah-ma grasps my hand. "You're a good girl, and a smart one at that. If others are doing it and it's allowed, then no one should dare tell my tsa-bóo-sun otherwise," she says with a huff.

"But there aren't a lot of people like me or Vivian who play this kind of music. What if I look silly up onstage?"

"Humph. Your grandfather didn't care about that, and you shouldn't, either. Plus, you won't look silly to me. That's impossible!" She shakes her head and her updo jiggles as usual.

The tightness in my chest loosens up. Somehow, Ah-ma always knows how to say the right things to make me feel a bit better.

And the fact that my ah-gong loved to play guitar feels special. Mom and Dad listen to music a lot, but I've never seen them pick up an instrument.

In fact, they made it clear the other night that I should

have started learning a long time ago to make it "worthwhile." But Ah-gong did it because he liked it. And according to Ah-ma's story, he started playing because he had a chance to, not because he had any particular goal.

I decide to listen to Ah-ma, not Marcos Alvarez. If she thinks I can rock out like Pearl Jam does, like Ah-gong did, then it's up to me to prove her right.

"Okay, Ah-ma. I do want to go to that summer camp. I want to learn how to play the electric guitar, too."

In an instant, my fingers start to itch, like they're looking for guitar strings to strum.

"Good." Ah-ma grunts, patting me on the shoulder. "There's my Lily. So tell me more about this camp."

I explain that registration is due in a little over a month and that friends and family can attend the performance at the end of camp.

"That sounds like a lot of fun," Ah-ma agrees.

"But the problem is Mom and Dad don't seem super excited about the idea of me going to a summer camp." Then it occurs to me that I'm talking to someone who has a lot of influence over my parents. Vivian's, too.

So I cup my sticky hands together and give her the best begging, please-please-pretty-please-with-a-cherry-on-top face I can. "Vivian and I really, really want to go to this. Ah-ma, can you help convince our parents to let us?"

Ah-ma chuckles. "Ah, you want to use me, eh?"

I grin at her teasing. "I guess . . . kind of?"

Ah-ma leans against the table. "How about this, Lily? I like the idea of you doing something that you're passionate about. But in exchange for my help, promise me you'll help Vivian more with her school work."

"I already do, Ah-ma," I say. "We spent most of last weekend at the library together, remember?"

"Do more. Look through her assignments or read to her and help her translate all those English words into Chinese. She should be doing better than she is." Ah-ma tsks, shaking her head.

"But what if she doesn't want my help?"

"Insist on it. You're her biǎo jiě, remember?"

How can I forget?

I'm not sure there's more I can do to help Vivian, though. I already got her an extra week, and Principal Klein refusing to help Marcos's cousin means there's no way she's going to say yes to me.

But I nod anyway. For Camp Rock Out.

"Deal?" Ah-ma says, holding out her sticky, flour-covered hand.

I grin and grasp it with mine. "Deal."

Phase One of Camp Rock Out sequence: initiated.

CHAPTER
12

BY THE TIME AH-MA AND I finish making all the plump meatball buns, Dad and Mom have both gotten home from work and prepared dinner. It's taken an entire hour to pinch every bun tightly closed, and my fingers are slightly tender from the effort.

I don't mind, though. It's probably going to feel like this when I start playing a real guitar. Guitar strings are made of steel, and to play chords, you have to press down on them with one hand while you strum with the other. I bet it takes a lot of finger strength and coordination to do all that.

I can't wait to try.

When I settle into my spot at the dinner table, though, nerves start to bubble in my belly. This time, I know the answer I want. I need Mom and Dad to say yes to Camp Rock Out, or else I'm never going to get to experience what playing a guitar actually feels like.

Or how it feels to rock out in front of a big crowd, with everyone screaming your name.

Dad passes out bowls of white rice and waves at the big plate on the table. "Hope you're hungry. I made us pái gǔ fàn tonight."

My mouth waters at the sight of crispy pork slices glistening with a sheen of oil. Ah-ma picks up the biggest piece with her chopsticks and places it on my plate. "For you, tsa-bóo-sun. For your strength in your goal today," Ah-ma whispers, winking. She waggles her head up and down in that headbanging way.

I take a bite to hide my giggles. Ah-ma always knows how to calm me down.

"Well, I've got something exciting to share," Dad announces.

"You do?" Ah-ma says, her mouth full of rice. "What is it, son?"

Mom reaches over and puts her hands on Dad's, and he smiles proudly back at her. "My boss has officially put me up for promotion," Dad says, his face flushing slightly. "I will meet the hiring committee next week."

"That's great, Dad!" I cheer. Ah-ma claps her hands, too.

"It's pretty exciting. Even being considered is quite an honor," Dad says.

"What about that idea you have? Did you decide to tell your boss's boss about it?" I ask.

Dad glances at Ah-ma and shakes his head. "No, I decided that it was too risky. I think Ma's right. There's no need to stir the pot during this delicate time. It won't make my boss look good, and I can't risk that right now. If Mr. Williams promotes me, I'll keep exploring it from my position as a new leader at the company."

Ah-ma nods. "I'm sure he will appreciate that. It shows you're a team player."

I'm not so sure, though. If his idea is going to help the company, won't that show initiative, that he's willing to speak up for what he thinks is right?

"Hey, Dad?" I ask hesitantly.

"Yeah, Lily?"

"Your idea is a good one, right?"

Dad chuckles. "Yes, it's a good one. And it'll work."

"Maybe you should stand up for it. It might even help you get the job."

Dad puts his chopsticks down and wipes his mouth with a napkin. "There's a time and place for everything, Lily. There are ways to get what we want by waiting for the right moment. Speaking up can get us into situations we don't want to be in."

My seat suddenly feels harder than normal. As much

as I want Dad to stand up for his idea, I actually get what he's saying. Marcos not getting Principal Klein's help with his cousin this afternoon meant it wasn't the right moment for me to speak up, either.

But how do I know when it is?

I'm not going to ask Dad and Ah-ma that question tonight, though. I need to save my energy for the one that really matters.

I take a deep breath. Time to go for it.

"I have an update, too," I announce, "about the summer camps we discussed with Auntie and Uncle the other night."

"Ah yes." Mom helps herself to another piece of pái gŭ. "What did you find out, Lily?"

"There's one that Vivian and I want to go to. It's a music camp that lasts four weeks. It's called Camp Rock Out."

Mom's eyebrows shoot up. "Rock Out? You mean, like rock and roll? You and Vivian playing that kind of music?"

Like a bolt of lightning, Ah-ma speaks up. "Wouldn't that be something, our kids up on a stage and playing music like that? We'd never see that in Taipei."

Woo-hoo, Ah-ma to the rescue!

Mom's face of skepticism turns into surprise. "Ma, this is something you support?"

"Yes." Ah-ma holds her head high. "The girls work so

hard, and they can do anything they put their minds to. The music they love is in this style, and as long as they follow the rules of this music, I don't see a problem with it. In fact, I think it's good they have a chance to have some fun."

Ah-ma totally gets it.

Although the part she said about "following the rules" sparks a tinge of annoyance in me. Are there rules in grunge? I'm not so sure.

"Hm," Dad says, frowning in that way he does when he's seriously thinking about something. "I do like the idea of Lily up onstage."

"I don't know. What if that time could be better spent doing something else?" Mom wonders out loud.

My heart starts to sink. Mom's the last one standing in my way. . . .

Then an idea flashes into my head—a way to get what we all want.

"How about we make a deal? Progress reports are coming up. If Vivian and I both get good grades, it means we've done what we're supposed to do, right?" I say.

The adults nod their heads in unison.

"How about if our progress reports come in and we've done well, we get to go to Camp Rock Out?" In my heart, I'm not sure it's a fair trade, because I'm doing fine. But this might be what Mom needs to make sure I know what's important.

To her, that is.

Plus, Vivian's been studying *so* hard these days. With my help and that extra essay time from Mr. Silvers, it's going to pay off, I'm sure.

Silence follows, and my pounding heart beats like a heavy percussion riff.

Finally, Mom speaks. "All right, I'm okay with that. But don't let anything distract you from those grades until they come in."

I let out the breath I didn't know I was holding. "Thanks, Mom! Will you talk to Auntie and Uncle about the camp and the grades, too?"

Dad takes a sip of his tea. "I'll do it. I'm sure your aunt will be fine with this, and it might be good motivation for Vivian to stay focused on her schoolwork."

She's plenty focused already, I want to say. But then my stomach unexpectedly churns.

Is Vivian going to be okay with this deal I'm making? She's under so much pressure already from Ah-ma and her parents. Will adding the chance to go to Camp Rock Out in exchange for better grades add fuel to the fire?

But I bite my tongue. I'm so close to getting what I want. Plus, I'm sure she'll understand. Vivian wants to go to Camp Rock Out as badly as I do.

Although she did say bǔ xí bān this summer could help her a lot, too. . . .

Ah-ma squeezes my hand. "I look forward to seeing

you up onstage with that guitar, tsa-bóo-sun." She leans in closer. "Your ah-gong would have loved to see it, too."

The image of me under bright stage lights with an electric guitar in hand makes whatever bit of doubt about Vivian and Camp Rock Out vanish from my mind. I beam excitedly back. "I can't wait."

I'm a big step closer to my transformation now.

Or more like, a progress grade closer.

CHAPTER
13

AFTER I SCARF DOWN DINNER, I head to the hallway, grab the phone from the side table, and pull it into my room. Then I close my bedroom door as much as I can while leaving it open enough for the phone cord to snake through the crack at the bottom.

If I win Student of the Year again this year, I'm going to ask my parents for my very own phone. There's one at the electronics store that's made of clear plastic, and you can see all the colorful components inside, like a big red bell or the green circuit board with different colored nodes. When you pick the receiver up, the teal pad behind the numbers lights up. Even the cord is a fun rainbow spiral.

Until that happens, though, if I want to talk privately,

my only option is to bring the boring hallway phone into my room, then balance on the edge of my bed just right so I can talk with the door mostly closed.

I rotate the dial to the number I want and let it spin back to the beginning before twisting it again to the next one.

Vivian answers right away. "Hello?"

"Biǎo mèi!" I exclaim. "I did it! I asked Mom and Dad about Camp Rock Out and they said yes! Dad promised that he'd talk to your parents, too. All we need to do is get good progress grades, and they'll sign us up. Isn't that great?" I wait breathlessly for Vivian to squeal with excitement.

But there's only silence from her side of the phone.

"Viv? You still there?" I say. "Everything okay?"

I hear a rustling on my cousin's side of the phone, like she's plopped down on her bed.

"I'm glad your parents are on board with us going to Camp Rock Out," Vivian finally says. "Especially for you, because you love this music so much. But to have it all depend on our progress grades? Wǒ bù zhī dào, biǎo jiě. What did Mr. Silvers say about helping me with English lit?"

"He said he can't give you any special tutoring," I admit. "But he did give you an extra week to turn in your essay. For the rest of us, it's due next Monday, but you've got till the Monday after."

"Oh, great. That'll help, for sure," Vivian says. But I can hear the faintest note of disappointment in her voice.

"I was hoping the school would be able to do more, but Principal Klein seems pretty set on not making any changes," I say. "Apparently, you're what's called an ESL student—English as a Second Language. Mr. Silvers said that schools in California used to have special classes to teach kids like you English, with real trained teachers. But they don't do that anymore after some law passed a few years ago."

"I didn't realize that there was a label for me," Vivian says. "Too bad about that law, huh?"

"Yeah. But, Vivian, you're studying so much already! With that extra week, you'll be fine," I try to reassure her.

"Maybe. I'm trying so hard, but it's not easy. What if I let you down?"

"That won't happen! How can you even think that?" I admonish her.

But inside my head, I cringe. Maybe I was wrong. Maybe I did make things worse for her with this deal I made.

At the same time, though, maybe a teeny tiny bit of extra pressure from her biǎo jiě will make a difference. I mean, it's got to click for her eventually. She's been able to do well in her studies back in Taipei, no problem.

Vivian sighs loudly. "You never know. There's still so much I don't understand in the story that I can't even start on the essay yet."

I wrap the phone cord around my fingers and watch the tips turn purple. Then I release the cord, and they turn back into their normal pink again.

The extra essay time doesn't seem to be enough for her to feel better about everything.

Take care of your biǎo mèi, Ah-ma's voice says in my head. *Do more.*

"Why don't you come over tomorrow after school? We can work on our homework together, and I can answer any questions you might have about the book."

"Okay," Vivian says softly. "Thanks, Lily. I better go." She hangs up quickly.

I stare at the phone, then get up to return it to the hallway table. Back in my room, I throw my arm over my eyes and flop backward onto my bed. Maybe this isn't such a good idea after all.

But as I land, something hard pokes me from behind.

I roll over and fumble around the bedsheets. When my fingers brush up against a hard, square shape, I grab at it.

It's my Temple of the Dog album. It must have fallen out of my backpack this morning.

Yeah, this feels like the right moment for some gloomy grunge music.

I pop open the jewel case and slide the CD into my stereo. "Hunger Strike" starts, and as the opening chords start in a slow, steady rhythm, I grimace as I think about how I could have done more this afternoon to get Vivian the help she wants. Instead, I chickened out.

Like usual.

If I had gone to Camp Rock Out last summer, I bet I would have had the courage to ask Principal Klein for ESL support today. I mean, getting up onstage and baring everything in front of an audience has got to be the best practice for speaking up in front of someone as important as she is. I might even have had the guts to say something to Marcos when he laughed at the idea of girl rockers.

I *need* to get to Camp Rock Out this summer.

And it's gotta be with Vivian, my future drummer.

Then, right as Eddie's and Chris's powerful voices join together and start crooning about how they'd take from the powerful but not the powerless, it hits me.

One of the coolest things about Temple of the Dog is that they're a temporary band that got together one time to honor a friend's memory. Chris Cornell was the front man for Soundgarden, and Jeff Ament and Stone Gossard were in a different band called Mother Love Bone. But that didn't matter. What mattered was that they cared about the same person and wanted to make music for him. So they got together and recorded an album.

Maybe I can help my cousin feel better about her schoolwork if I join forces with other kids who care about the same thing I do. Kids with family and friends who need ESL help, like Vivian.

Kids like Marcos Alvarez. Like Yoona Kim. Marcos's cousin is having trouble with English, too, and Yoona tutors a bunch of Korean kids.

But would they be up for figuring this out together? They barely know me. Plus, Marcos was a jerk about the whole girls at Camp Rock Out thing. Do I really want to be around him more?

Vivian needs me, though. Plus, Ah-ma expects me to do more as the older sister cousin. While going to the principal isn't something me or anyone in my family is going to do, figuring this out with other Pacific Park Middle kids can't be that hard.

And it's important enough for me to try.

It might be time for me to finally form my own band.

CHAPTER
14

WHEN I PUSH OPEN THE glass doors of the Pacific Park Middle library, I notice right away that it's quieter today than usual, probably because it's after school instead of the middle of the day.

Or maybe it seems that way because I can hear my own heart beating.

Last night, I dusted off the printed school directory we get at the beginning of every school year and looked up Marcos's and Yoona's phone numbers. But I hadn't called anyone besides Vivian in a long time, and it took a lot of effort to control the waver in my voice when they each picked up.

After I told them I wanted to ask them about something, Yoona and Marcos each said they'd come meet me today. But what if one of them has a change of heart?

As I walk past the circulation desk, though, I spot them right away, sitting next to each other at a table in the corner.

My heart swells. They showed up.

They're actually leaning toward each other, their heads moving to the same beat. In fact, they're sharing a set of earphones, listening to something on Yoona's Walkman.

When I reach the table, Yoona greets me, her blue glasses glinting and her curly hair tied back in a ponytail with a neon-green tie-dyed scrunchie. "Hey, Lily. I was introducing Marcos to Seo Taiji and Boys, that Korean group I told you about in class the other day."

"I had no idea that Korean music could sound like that," Marcos says.

Yoona grins. "Well, their music is really different from what you'd typically hear in Seoul these days. But I have a feeling their style of pop and dance is going to be big."

Marcos nods approvingly. "Yeah, they're pretty sick. I dig it."

I can't help but grin. Music really does bind people together, no matter where they're from or who they are.

"By the way, have you listened to the Smashing Pumpkins album yet?" Marcos turns his attention to me.

"Not yet," I admit. "But I will tonight, promise."

"So, Lily, what's up?" Yoona peers at me with a curious look on her face. "Why did you ask us to come here today?"

I take a seat and clasp my hands in front of me on the table. "So . . . I was hoping to get your help with something."

Marcos adjusts his baseball cap, scrunching it farther down his floppy hair. "My help? What does Ms. Student of the Year need from someone like me?"

I ignore the tinge of annoyance at being called that. And I can feel the seed of doubt he planted yesterday about Camp Rock Out take deeper root.

But I do my best to ignore it.

I have a mission to accomplish.

"Yoona, I've seen you tutoring Korean kids, and Marcos, I know you've been trying to get help for your cousin, too."

"Yeah, I actually have a session here in a few minutes," Yoona says.

"Have you been tutoring for a while?" I ask. "Is it working?"

"Well, I do my best." Yoona crinkles her nose as she pushes her glasses up. "Honestly, I'm trying to figure it out as I go. I don't know what to do aside from having them do writing exercises and grammar worksheets."

"That's better than me. My cousin moved here from Taiwan six months ago, and she's still not feeling very confident about her English. I tried to ask Mr. Silvers for help, but he said he couldn't do anything."

Marcos chimes in. "Yeah, I asked him, too. He said that I had to talk to Principal Klein, which I did." He shakes his head, looking annoyed. "Lily saw what happened. It was a big no from her. She thinks Pacific Park Middle needs to be 'English first.'" He gestures with exaggerated air quotes when he says "English first." "You talked to her after me, right, Lily? What did she say when you asked for help for your cousin?"

I avoid his eyes. "Um, actually, I didn't ask. It wouldn't have mattered, anyway," I mumble.

Marcos sweeps the hair out of his eyes with a frustrated swipe. "This would be way easier if the school knew how many kids need the extra attention. Then maybe Principal Klein would do more."

"But she doesn't know." Yoona's voice sounds a bit higher than normal.

This is the perfect setup. So I go for it. "Let me tell you my idea."

They both turn to me with expectant eyes, and my palms get clammy. This is a super small audience, but it's an audience nonetheless.

And Robot Lily does not do well in these circumstances.

Come on, Lily! Go for it and be grunge.

I take a deep breath and swallow down my nervousness. "What if we did something about it ourselves? What if the three of us started something like an ESL homework club, where we meet somewhere after school to help our family and friends with their schoolwork?"

"A homework club?" Yoona raises her eyebrows up high. "Hmm, that's interesting."

"We could meet somewhere fun, like the café of Power Records after school once or twice a week. Kids can bring their homework, and the three of us will help as much as we can," I suggest. "That way, there's strength in numbers, and we could learn what works or not from each other."

"Do you think us helping will make a difference, though?" Marcos scrunches up his face in skepticism. "We're just kids like they are."

"I dunno." I shrug. "But it's worth a try, don't you think?"

"Yeah, that's true. Okay, I'm down," Marcos says, crossing his hands behind his head. "I'm sure Carlos will be up for this, too. When do you want to start?"

Mr. Silvers said that progress grades will be mailed home in about two weeks, which isn't that far away. Vivian's got to get her confidence up fast.

"How about we get together on Tuesday afternoon, after school? Teachers usually hand the week's assignments out on Mondays and Tuesdays, and we can work on those together," I suggest. Marcos and Yoona both nod.

"I'll bring copies of the worksheets I've been using for tutoring. It's a place to start," Yoona adds.

I lean back in my chair and smile gratefully at them. "Thanks," I say. "Vivian will appreciate all this."

And now, my cousin will finally get the help she needs. It's not real "certified teacher" ESL support, like Pacific Park Middle used to have before that proposition was passed.

But it's better than nothing.

I call Vivian when I get home, and she comes over so we can do our homework together. After she says hello to Ah-ma and we retreat into my bedroom, I tell her about the ESL Homework Club and how Yoona, Marcos, and their friends are going to meet us next Tuesday at Power Records for our first session.

Vivian's eyes widen into big anime eyes. "Zhēn de? There are other kids who need help like me?" she says in Mandarin.

I nod. "You're not the only one, Vivian."

She seems relieved, and I pat myself on the back for my brilliant idea.

See, all she needs is to know she's not alone. Vivian will be fine.

We spend the rest of the afternoon working on homework assignments. When there's a word or phrase she doesn't understand, I do my best to explain it to her in Chinese. But the vocabulary is pretty advanced, and I don't know how to say "tenant" or "suspicious" in Chinese.

I jot down every word Vivian has trouble with onto a separate piece of paper and add the dictionary definition. Like Mr. Silvers said, *The Westing Game* is required reading for every seventh grader, no matter how good their English is. This vocab list might come in handy for the other ESL Homework Club kids.

Meanwhile, as she reads, I pull out my social studies textbook and flip it to the chapter about the women's suffrage movement. Our presentation is due next Friday, and we had agreed as a group to individually research the different tactics the women suffragettes used in their fight for the right to vote. Then we'd compare notes and figure out which ones to present to the class.

Everything I'm reading about that time of American history reminds me of grunge music. The suffragettes were angry and rebellious and demanded what they thought was fair, which a lot of Eddie Vedder's lyrics do, too. The suffragettes got people to sign petitions to prove how many other people cared about giving women the right to vote, then presented them to the authorities. They also ran marches, dropped pamphlets from the sky, and wrote satirical poems to get more people to see what was happening.

I bet the suffragettes would have insisted that girls could be grunge rockers, too. Even Taiwanese American seventh graders like me and Vivian.

By the time we've finished our homework for the day, it's late afternoon and Ah-ma insists Vivian stay for dinner. Ah-ma steams a few bah-oâns, grills some sausage with raw garlic, and stir-fries a bunch of a-choy. During dinner, Dad goes on and on about calculating packet rates so he could reprogram the computers at Compu-Scape, and Mom and Ah-ma exchange notes on the latest gossip in the Taiwanese community. It sounds like college acceptance letters have been coming in, and they go through which Taiwanese or Chinese high school senior has been accepted into which Ivy League. Mom volleys not-so-subtle hints at me and Vivian about which colleges are good and what it takes to get into one.

Vivian and I exchange eye rolls when my parents aren't watching. We're still years away from needing to worry about any of this!

After dinner, while the adults head into the living room to sip on tea and snack on roasted watermelon seeds, Vivian and I escape to my bedroom again.

This time, though, the schoolbooks aren't coming out.

I shut the door firmly behind me, bounce to my nightstand, and pull out Marcos's Smashing Pumpkins CD. "Look what I have, biǎo mèi!"

"Ooh, a new album? Ràng wǒ kàn kàn!" Vivian exclaims. We jump onto my bed to inspect the cover art together.

The words "Smashing Pumpkins" are written on top of a circle made up of what look like red jewels. Below it is the album name, *Gish*, and inside the circle are who I assume are the band members. One guy has his hands raised up high, like he's reaching for the top of the camera lens. There's also a girl with long blond hair in a black dress, and on her right is a guy with long black hair . . . and he's Asian. "Look, Vivian," I say, pointing. "He's like us."

"Neat!" she says. "Let's hear it."

The first track starts off in typical rock fashion, with a steady percussion joined a few bars in by the distorted riffs of the rhythm guitar. But when the vocalist starts singing, we look at each other in surprise.

The vocalist's voice is high-pitched and dreamy—the total opposite of Eddie's deep baritone. But there's still that rough edge that makes it grunge.

Different yet familiar.

"I like it!" Vivian declares. "Where'd you get this, anyway?"

"Marcos Alvarez lent it to me," I confess, avoiding Vivian's eyes.

"Oh yeah?" She looks at me closely, and I can't help but blush slightly.

Luckily, my biǎo mèi knows me well enough not to tease me about a boy. "Well, that's nice of him," she says.

"Yeah, kinda. But he also said girls like us have never shown up at Camp Rock Out before. And he's gone a few summers already." I fiddle with the corner of my pillow, the smoothness of the seams soft against my fingers.

Vivian shrugs. "You'll be the first. You'll show them how awesome girl rockers can be."

This is exactly why I need Vivian with me at Camp Rock Out. Her confidence is infectious.

I grin at her and toss the pillow in her direction. "Geez, biǎo mèi, why can't you be this sure about your schoolwork?"

She catches it before it hits her in the face, laughing. "Hey, quit it!"

Then I pause for a minute, thinking about what Vivian said. "But you meant *we'll* be the first, right? Not just me."

"Huh?" Vivian looks confused as she hugs the pillow to her knees.

"You just said that I'd be the first one at Camp Rock

Out. But you meant that the two of us would prove those boys wrong, didn't you?"

"Right, yeah," she mutters. "The two of us."

"Okay, good." I nod. "And you're right. I don't think what he said should stop us from going. But I bet the boys will be paying a lot of attention to how well we play."

"Hm, maybe." Vivian shrugs. "But who cares?"

"I do!" I insist. "I was thinking, now that we've got some things going to make sure our grades are good, maybe we can think about how we could get a head start on learning how to play rock. It probably won't be that hard for you with drums, Vivian. You need two sticks and something to bang on to practice rhythms."

Vivian's face lights up, and she rummages through her backpack. She pulls out a pair of chopsticks. "I can use these!" she says with a big laugh, tapping on my bedspread, her eyes twinkling.

"Ha, that's perfect!" I giggle. "But make sure they're clean! You could flip a laundry basket or garbage can upside down and bang on those, too."

Vivian nods. "Exactly."

Percussion, check.

"What about me, though? An electric guitar is way harder to improvise." I scrunch up my nose in thought.

Sure, I daydream about being a rock star like Eddie

all the time. But I've never actually laid my hands on a real electric guitar before. And I don't know anyone in the Taiwanese community who might have one lying around that I can borrow.

Plus, there's the other stuff you need, like an amplifier to transmit the music or distortion pedals to give it that gritty sound.

My eyes scan the room, looking for things I could use to improvise as a guitar. As they skim over my desk, they land on something bright yellow.

It's a Power Records bag.

I leap to my feet. "I got it. Keiko. She knows how to play grunge, and she's an amazing guitarist. She even has her own band and everything."

"Dāng rán! Keiko is so cool! She'll probably show us a thing or two if we ask nicely." Vivian claps her hands together in excitement.

"Perfect! Keiko usually works in the afternoons, so we can ask her on Friday after school."

Vivian flashes me a thumbs-up. "Hǎo jì huà!"

I grin excitedly back. Yay, we have a plan! And a good one, too. The best person to teach us about grunge music is someone who represents who I want to be when I grow up. Keiko is *so* grunge.

Later, alone in my bed as I stare up at the ceiling, I think about how much closer Camp Rock Out feels. I've stepped up to get Vivian more help with extra essay time and the ESL club, *and* we might have the chance to learn how to play even before Camp Rock Out starts.

Maybe my transformation will start earlier than I thought.

I can't wait.

CHAPTER
15

AFTER SCHOOL ON FRIDAY, VIVIAN and I hop onto our bikes and head toward Power Records. When we get there, Keiko's sorting through receipts at the information desk. Her hair is tied up in a high ponytail, and she's got a leather jacket over a black crop top. Her red-and-black checkered pants match the red boots with black laces on her feet.

"Hi, Keiko!" I call out.

She looks up from her receipts. "Hey, Lily and Vivian! Here for more music? We have a new batch of used CDs."

"Actually, we came to ask for your help," I say as boldly as I can.

Keiko's eyebrows pop up. "Oh? What can I do for you?"

I swing my backpack forward and pull out the Camp

Rock Out flyer. "Vivian and I want to go to this summer camp."

Keiko takes it and skims it quickly. "Wow, this is too cool! It's perfect for you two." She hands the flyer back to me, and I fold it up neatly before returning it to my backpack.

"So how can I help?" she asks.

"The flyer says we can sign up as beginners, but Vivian and I were thinking it might be fun to get a head start by learning how to play a little before camp begins. We don't want to show up totally unprepared and play terribly right away. We might be the only girls there."

"Music is about playing with your heart. As long as you do that, you'll be fine," Keiko reassures me. "You don't need to prove yourself to anyone before you get there. It's not your job to combat other people's stereotypes. Showing up is enough."

I'm not so sure, though. I don't want to look bad in front of other people, especially if they already expect me to fail.

But Keiko hasn't taken the bait I've laid out for her and offered to help us with some lessons. I look at Vivian with pleading eyes. She'll know what to say to get what we want.

Vivian nods back at me, then turns to Keiko. "Um, we know nothing about how to play," Vivian says. "It will be fun if we try. Bài tuō?" She slips into Mandarin again, but there's no mistaking what Vivian's asking for.

Keiko inspects us closely, her lips curling slightly upward. I hold my breath. Will she . . . ?

"Of course I'll help! We need as many young rockers like you as we can get!" she exclaims, laughing.

Whew. She's in.

My heart is about to burst with excitement.

Then Keiko furrows her eyebrows. "Okay, so what instruments are you hoping to learn at the camp? That'd be a good place to start so I can think about what to teach you two."

Without thinking, I blurt out, "I want to sing like Eddie Vedder." Then my face flushes like a ripe tomato.

Eek, where did that come from? The idea of me singing like Eddie, with his intense and powerful voice . . . How could a robot like me possibly sound like that?

"I mean, um, I want to play the electric guitar. Yeah, that's it." I backtrack before Keiko has a chance to laugh at me. "And Vivian's always wanted to play percussion."

Keiko smiles at me gently. "Playing the guitar is a ton of fun. Joan's the lead vocalist of our band, Pandora's Box. She can give you some singing pointers, too, if you want."

"Oh, no, I couldn't do vocals." I shake my head. "That's not me."

"You can be whoever you want to with music! That's

the freedom of rock and roll. How about you try both and see which you like better?"

My tomato face is about to burst into flames at the idea of me at the mic.

I couldn't.

"I just want to be able to play music like Pearl Jam," I fumble, hoping Keiko lets it go.

Keiko laughs. "I totally get it. Pearl Jam *is* pretty sick." She looks at me for a second before continuing. "But, you know, none of them set out to be rock stars. Take Eddie, for example. His lyrics and sound are amazing because he sings about things he cares about. Learning how other people play or trying to follow a certain music style are good places to start. But eventually, you need to find your own sound, depending on what it is you want to say to the world."

I nod, although I'm not quite sure what Keiko means. Pearl Jam's music is pretty much perfect. If I get anywhere close to sounding like them, I'll be the happiest girl ever.

"So how do we begin?" I want my transformation to start ASAP.

Keiko clips the receipts together with a red stapler. "Hm, how about this? You two can come to one of my band practices, and Joan and I will show you a few things."

My heart jumps. "Wow, that'd be so awesome! I've never seen live music played by real rockers before."

Come to think of it, I've never seen an all-girl rock band, either.

Keiko chuckles. "Real rockers, huh? Anyone can be a rocker. You only need something to say and the guts to say it." She taps her finger to her chin, like she's thinking about something. "Actually, Lily, I have something that could help you get started right away."

I follow her to the steel lockers in the corner, and Keiko twists a silver lock on one door. It opens with a clang, and she rummages inside before pulling out a dog-eared book.

"I keep this around to remind me of where I started," Keiko says, thumbing through it with a nostalgic look on her face. "It's an instructional electric guitar book that covers a lot of the basics. This might be a good start before you meet with me and Joan and the rest of the band."

The book has a black cover with a picture of a single electric guitar on it. The words "Electric Guitar Basics: For the Beginner" are printed across the top in yellow.

I flip it open, past the table of contents, to a page that has drawings of different types of guitars. I recognize one right away. Mike McCready's is like that, with the edges of the body curling up like a manta ray.

Fender Stratocaster.

The next one looks like the one I've seen Stone Gossard play.

Gibson Les Paul.

My heart beats faster as I read the names of the guitar parts.

Headboard. Nut. Neck. Strings. Frets. Pickups.

The new words soak into my brain, and my fingers start to tingle. "This is great. Thank you, Keiko." I hug the book to my chest like it's a new Xiǎo Dīng Dāng manga.

"No problem. Borrow it for as long as you'd like. Take this, too." She pulls out two CDs from behind the information desk and hands one to me and one to Vivian. "This is the demo album of our band. You might want to listen to it before you come to one of our practices so you can get a sense of our sound." Keiko takes a piece of paper off the desk and scribbles an address on it. "Here's where our band practices, in Joan's garage. We'll be there on Monday from around four to sevenish in the evening. Come by and the band will show you girls a few things."

"Thank you so much, Keiko!" I take the paper and CD with both my hands, like she's giving me a red envelope for Lunar New Year. Vivian drops hers in her bag, and we wave goodbye.

As I head out the doors of Power Records, I grin to myself.

Things are changing already. I can feel it.

* * *

Later that night, I start working on my English lit essay. Vivian's got a whole extra week, thanks to me, but I don't, and it's due in a few days. So I hunker down and follow the essay structure that Mr. Silvers taught us, starting with a thesis statement, then at least three supporting points, each accompanied by a few quotes from the book to serve as evidence.

By the time I've gotten the overall outline done, there's a few more minutes before bedtime. Time to relax a bit before calling it a day.

Which means it's music time! On my listening schedule today is Pacific Park's one and only all-girl grunge band, Pandora's Box. I pull out Keiko's album from my backpack and study the cover art closely.

In the center is a drawing of a treasure chest with its lid wide open, and a bunch of monsters are flying out of it, like they're escaping from the box. Each monster has a girl's face on it, who I assume are the band members. Their expressions are wicked and fierce and strong. Keiko's monster has snakes on its head, like Medusa, and she looks like she's ready to take over the world, no matter what.

I slide the CD into my stereo and crank up the volume as it whirls to life. The first track kicks off with an impressively fast percussion riff and Joan's powerful voice, both hitting full volume right away.

Hey, hey, hey, I'm not who you want me to be.
Hey, hey, hey, I'm all who I want to be.

I close my eyes to absorb every beat. With the fast-paced tempo and loud, distorted riffs, I can hear bits of Nirvana's punk rock vibe in Pandora's Box's style. But the guitar riffs have a fuzzy, heavy-metal edge to them, and Joan croons about girl power and not wanting to conform to society's expectations of what feminism means.

It strikes me that grunge rock vocals in a girl's voice sound very different from what I'm used to. Joan's pitch is higher and brighter than Eddie's or Chris Cornell's.

But Pandora's Box's sound holds the same power and passion as those other bands.

So.

Amazingly.

Cool.

I need to figure out how to play as quickly as I can so I can sound like them.

First things first, though. I need something that will help me practice finger work from now until Camp Rock Out. I have a feeling that figuring out where my fingers need to be for all the different chords is going to take longer than a practice session or two with Keiko.

Asking my parents for a real electric guitar is out of the question. There's no way we have money lying around for something as unimportant in their minds as that.

I have to work harder and smarter. As Ah-ma always says: *It's good to be resourceful.*

If I can't have a real guitar, maybe I can make one. Because sometimes you have to fake it till you make it.

Maybe *that* should be my motto.

I pull Keiko's guitar instruction book out of my backpack and flip to the pages that show the parts of a guitar. It looks like where your left hand goes to make chords is called the fretboard, and the strips marked on it where your fingers go are called fret markers. To hit the most common chords, my fingers will need to move between a few fret markers. This means whatever fretboard I make needs to be long enough to fit three or four of them.

My eyes scan my bedroom looking for something, anything, that could work.

A clothes hanger? Nah. Too thin and not straight enough.

One of my manga books? Nope. Too wide and too short.

It's too bad Xiǎo Dīng Dāng can't pull a real guitar out of his cat belly pouch.

Then my eyes land on two wooden rulers sticking up from the coffee tins squatting on my desk that double as pencil holders.

Hmm. Maybe . . .

I leap up from my bed and grab them. One by itself is too narrow for the guitar strings it'll need. But two side by side and laid flat could be perfect. I find a roll of masking tape in a desk drawer and tape the rulers together. I curl the fingers of my left hand around them.

It's the perfect width.

Next are the fret markers. With a black Sharpie, I mark four horizontal lines across the top half for the fret markers.

Now I need strings. Six, to be exact.

When I yank open the last desk drawer, a ball of pink rubber bands rolls forward.

Score.

I manage to get six of them to stretch across the entire length of my fake guitar neck. I run my fingers across them gently . . . and there's a faint *twang* sound. I press my finger on different strings to see if the sound changes as I "play."

Nope, not really.

The sound that comes from what's in my hands is a long way off from the intense richness of what comes from a real electric guitar. But it's good enough for now.

With my makeshift guitar, I circle through the power chords that the book explains are important to learn. E minor, C major, A major. Then I do them again.

By the time Dad knocks on my door to remind me that it's time for bed, I can switch between the basic chords pretty easily, although I have to refer to the instruction book for the right notes. But I can't get my fingers to hold down more than three strings at once, and they're aching from the effort.

Still, there's a small ball of satisfaction in my stomach. I have a feeling Eddie would approve of my little guitar. Pearl Jam is nothing fancy, either. Just amazingly good.

I hope with all my might that this little guitar will make me amazingly good, too.

CHAPTER
16

OVER THE WEEKEND, I SPEND any free time I have practicing chords on my DIY guitar. I want to show up to Keiko's band practice with some of the chords memorized so I can hit the ground running when I finally have a real guitar in my hands.

Vivian comes over on Saturday and Sunday mornings so we can do homework together. The first session of the ESL Homework Club isn't until next Tuesday, and I do my best to help her work her way through *The Westing Game*'s complicated story. As for me, I mostly work on turning my English lit outline into strong sentences and convincing paragraphs.

By the time Monday rolls around, I've got the basic chord positions memorized by heart. I turn in my essay, and Vivian's only got three more chapters left before she finishes reading *The Westing Game* and can get started on hers. And the best part—Pandora's Box's band practice is today!

After the final bell rings, Vivian and I meet at the bike racks, then make our way to the address that Keiko wrote down for us. I pedal faster as Vivian and I cruise down Broadway on our way to Joan's house. As we turn a corner, a loud rhythm starts to pulse through the air. I catch Vivian's eye, and she grins at me as she stands up high on her bike.

Here we go!

The garage door of one of the squat yellow houses is wide open, and a girl with long chestnut-brown, black-tipped hair sings into a mic, her hands cupped around it and her voice coming through the speakers super smooth and rich. She must be Joan, their vocalist. Meanwhile, Keiko's jamming to Joan's right, the fingers of her left hand moving up and down the neck of her Fender Jaguar while her right strums the steel strings. A girl with short curly hair and huge hoop earrings bangs on the snares of a drum set as her head bounces vigorously to the heavy rhythm. The bass guitarist has almost the exact opposite energy as she stands still in one place, practically hiding behind a curtain of shoulder-length purple hair as her hand moves in a blur to the song's steady beat.

The band finishes the song right as Vivian and I hop off our bikes. We cheer and whoop as we push them up the driveway and park them off to the side. Keiko grins, takes the guitar off her shoulder, and places it on a stand.

"Hey, that was solid!" she says, turning toward her bandmates. "Let's end early today, though, so we can show these girls a thing or two." She waves us closer, and I shyly approach.

Vivian practically bounces into the garage, though, her bangs flopping up and down like the wings of a blackbird. "Tǐng kù de!"

"This is Joan." Keiko motions to the girl at the mic, and Joan flashes us a peace sign as she takes a sip of water from a bottle. "This is Tori, our drummer," Keiko continues, waving at the percussionist, "and this is Maia, our bassist. We're Pandora's Box, Pacific Park's one and only all-girl rock band! Hopefully we won't be the last, though." Keiko winks at us.

Tori twirls the drumsticks in her hands. "Keiko told us that you girls want to go to a rock camp this summer? That's so cool. I wish I had that kind of thing when I first started playing."

"Lily wants to try the guitar, and Vivian wants to play drums." Keiko nudges each of us forward as she introduces us.

"Sick!" Tori points her drumsticks at Vivian. "You

look like you've got nice arms to become a killer percussionist."

Vivian laughs and strikes a bodybuilder pose. "I strong and I play strong!" she says in her accented English.

The way Vivian is ready to dive in makes my chest puff up. She's not letting her English get in the way of her learning the drums.

"Okay, Lily, come with me, and Tori can show Vivian a few things," Keiko says.

Vivian joins Tori, and in no time at all, Tori is showing her how to hold the drumsticks. Keiko leads me to a few overturned crates in the driveway and lugs over an amplifier while Maia and Joan disappear into the house.

Keiko clasps her hands together. "Okay, let's start with what you know. Have you had a chance to look at that instruction book I lent you?"

"Yes!" I exclaim, excited to show off what I've learned over the last few days. I pull out my DIY guitar and hand it to Keiko. "I've even been practicing finger work on this."

"Oh my gosh, this is sick!" Keiko laughs, turning it around in her hands and putting her fingers in a few chord positions. "It's so clever of you to put something together in this way. It's very grunge to make do with what you have."

I beam with pride at her words. A real grunge rocker

is complimenting me. I feel like I could float away.

"All right, so you've got a good sense of the chords. How about I show you the gear?" She grabs her Fender Jaguar and plugs it into the amplifier. Keiko flips some switches on her guitar and twirls the knob before strumming a few chords. "Playing around with these guitar settings helps get that raw, distorted grunge rock sound you love so much," she explains. "There are a ton of settings on the amp, too." She makes some adjustments on the amplifier this time and strums again. The sound coming out of her guitar changes with each turn of the dials.

"All right, you try it now," Keiko says. She stands up to take the guitar strap off her shoulder and pull it tighter for my petite frame.

My heart pounds. It's time.

Keiko instructs me to sit on a crate, loops the strap around me, and gently lays the guitar on my lap.

The first thing I notice is how heavy it is. It's solid and strong, almost comforting. I curl my left fingers lightly over the guitar neck and place my right hand over the strings. They're thicker than I thought they'd be. I brush them gently with my fingertips, and they vibrate slightly under my touch. The motion of the strings pulses up through my arms and into my body.

I can feel myself changing already.

I look up at Keiko, and she's grinning at me. "Feels pretty awesome to finally hold one, huh? I can see how you feel from the expression on your face."

I blush. I had no idea I was so easy to read.

"Okay, let's play. Here, you can use this pick." Keiko hands me a small yellow plastic triangle. "Sounds like you know some basic power chords already. Let's start with E minor."

I place my fingers in the right position and pull the pick over the top string . . .

. . . and it flies out of my hand, bounces off my knee, and hits the ground a few inches away.

"Whoa! Ha, that's not supposed to happen," Keiko chuckles. She retrieves the pick and hands it back to me.

I take a deep breath and grasp the pick tighter between my fingers this time.

Twang . . .

There's a more recognizable sound this time, although it's nothing like the crisp chord it should sound like.

"I can tell that your finger positions are right, so all you need is a little practice strumming to get the right feel and sound. Why don't you do that for a bit on your own?" Keiko sets me up with headphones that plug straight into the amp. They do wonders to mute out Vivian's drumming, and having the sound come directly through the headphones frees me up to make mistakes that no one else can hear.

After a half hour, my T-shirt is soaked in sweat, and the tips of my fingers are tender from pushing down on the steel strings. But I *am* able to move between the frets in a somewhat smooth, fluid way, and I can strum a few clean chords.

Suddenly, I notice Keiko's in front of me, motioning at me to take off my headphones. "Come on, Lily, let's hear it."

I blush, but when I look around, it's only her and Vivian. The rest of the band members must be inside somewhere. I pull off the headphones and unplug them from the speaker. Then I play a few of the chords I'd been practicing.

"Lily, that sounds great! You're a fast learner. Vivian's doing pretty good over there, too." She motions toward the other side of the garage, where Vivian's short hair is flying as she drums away.

Joan enters the garage from inside the house, a few sodas in her hands. "Keiko, didn't you tell me that Lily wanted to try vocals, too?" Joan hands Keiko a drink. "I can set you up at the mic and show you a few things before we call it a day."

Eep. Keiko told her that I wanted to sing like Eddie Vedder?

I do my best to laugh off Joan's suggestion. "Oh, no,

it's okay. I've got enough to learn with the guitar," I say, waving my hand in the air to shoo away the idea of me at the mic.

Vivian calls out to me from her perch by the drums. "Shì shì kàn ba, biǎo jiě! Singing vocals will be so fun! Give it a shot."

Being more like Eddie Vedder *would* be so awesome. Or like Joan. People would notice me for sure.

For a split second, I start to move in the direction of the mic.

But the replay of my robot performance at the Student of the Year ceremony suddenly flashes into my head. It's one thing to play the guitar. But to be the one at the front of the band?

I shake my head. "No, I'm okay. Guitar is good enough for me."

"Come on, give it a try," Joan says, motioning toward the mic. "Here, we'll turn off the amplifier so it's less intimidating." She flips a switch on the amp that the mic is plugged into and adjusts the stand lower to my height. Joan is so certain that I'm afraid to say no again.

I get in front of the mic, my arms hanging awkwardly by my side. "Uh, what do I do?"

"Well, first things first. People think that singing rock is all about screaming and yelling into the mic as loud as you can."

"It's not?" I ask.

"Nope. Being a great rock vocalist isn't about forcing air through your throat. Instead, the air needs to start deep inside, from your soul, then move through your heart and out through your voice. That's what will help you project that strong, powerful sound that defines grunge."

Start with my soul? What does that even mean?

Joan has me do some breathing exercises to warm up. "Now let's have you try to sing something so I can get a sense of where you're starting from," Joan says. "Do you know Joan Jett's 'I Love Rock 'n' Roll'?"

Am I really going to sing out loud for other people to hear?

Joan doesn't bother waiting for me to respond. "Okay, Keiko, want to play the intro for us?"

"Sure," Keiko says, grinning. She switches seats with Vivian and holds a set of drumsticks up high. "Ready!"

Joan slings her guitar around her shoulder and gets into position. Keiko kicks off with the familiar start of the song, then Joan starts strumming. When it's time for vocals, I open my mouth . . .

And the words come out small and squeaky.

Ugh. Absolutely awful.

Joan raises her hand and Keiko stops drumming. "Lily, remember the breathing. The air comes from the chest, through the heart, and out through your voice."

Vivian cheers me on. "Jiā yóu, biǎo jiě!"

"Try to connect with what you feel and project that emotion into your voice. Don't worry about how good you sound. Focus on getting the passion and commitment out there," Joan says. "Imagine the words have fingers that reach the fans at the very back of the crowd."

I grimace. My actual fingers are trembling, so I'm pretty sure my voice isn't going to reach any farther.

"Take two." Joan signals to Keiko, who starts the intro again. I take a deep breath and imagine air coming from my chest to my head. *Be grunge*, I tell myself. *Connect with what you feel inside.*

But the only feeling inside me is doubt, and what comes out of my mouth is a whisper, not a growl.

"I can't do it." I shake my head and step away from the mic.

"It takes time and patience," Joan insists. "And conviction. You'll get there, Lily."

"No, I mean it. I can't do it." My face flushes red, and I resist the urge to book it down the street and get as far away from here as I can. Out of the corner of my eye, I see Vivian staring at me, worried.

Keiko gets up from her spot on the driveway. "You tried, Lily. That counts for a lot. And you're a total natural at the guitar." She waves at the street, and I'm surprised at how long the shadows have gotten. "Why don't we give you both a ride home?" Keiko suggests, motioning toward the red Chevrolet parked on the street. "Your bikes should fit in the back of my car."

I take a look at my watch, and, yikes, it's almost dinnertime. Ah-ma's waiting for me at home, and Mom and Dad will both be done with work soon. "Yes, please," I say politely. "A ride home would be great."

Vivian and I help Keiko stuff our bikes into the trunk of her Chevy, then we pile into the backseat. Joan scoots into the passenger side, and we wave goodbye to the other band members of the coolest girl grunge band ever.

At least until Vivian and I get good enough to start our own.

CHAPTER
17

AS WE DRIVE THROUGH THE streets of Pacific Park, the early evening light bouncing off the storefronts and cruising cars, my insides mix in a weird combination of pride and disappointment. Holding a real electric guitar in my hands felt so good, and all that practice on my silly DIY one actually paid off. Keiko even said that I am a total natural.

But on the other hand, I'm kicking myself for my utter failure as a vocalist. Something about getting in front of a mic makes me freeze, like a chicken stuck in a block of ice.

The guitar part was so amazing, though. And seeing Keiko, Joan, Tori, and Maia in action today totally blew my mind. Pandora's Box is as tough and strong as the all-boy bands that rule the grunge scene these days. Seeing Keiko, who's got a face like mine, rocking out with a guitar and doing the thing she loves fills my heart with such joy.

As we pass by Power Records, I think about Marcos Alvarez and the fact that no girl rockers have ever shown up at Camp Rock Out before. "Keiko, Joan, do you mind if I ask you a question?"

Keiko's eyes meet mine in the rearview mirror. "Go for it," she says.

"What made you decide to start a band in the first place? Especially an all-girl one?"

Keiko chuckles. "Well, for me, I fell in love with the music and wanted to play. I didn't plan on making an all-girl band . . . it kind of happened. I met Joan, who has this incredible voice, and Tori and Maia auditioned. We just clicked. We'd each been rejected a ton when we tried to join other bands. We decided to get together and create our own sound, something that's unique. Even though we're pretty different—Tori's studying to be a nurse, and Maia trained as a classical violinist—our styles somehow fit."

I look at Vivian, who's tapping out drumming rhythms on her knees. I wonder what it'd be like to meet a Tori or a Maia and have them join us. Then we could be a real rock band.

Or even better, a group of friends.

Joan speaks up. "We also work well as a band because we have similar things we want to say."

"Things you want to say?" I ask. "What do you mean?"

"Well, grunge music—or any kind of rock—isn't about being loud and angry for no reason. It's about speaking up and shining light into the dark corners that people don't like to see. Even though we get rejected a lot as female rockers, we don't want to hide what makes us special. We want the freedom to be who we are and express that however we wish to."

Keiko turns on the blinker and shifts lanes. "As Pandora's Box, we're hoping to change the industry, one song, one gig, at a time. The lyrics we write are about turning the patriarchy on its head."

"Yeah, I get that," I say softly. The suffragettes had their own way of speaking up and speaking out, too.

What do *I* want to say when I pick up an electric guitar, though?

"How do people react to your music? You don't see a lot of girl rock-and-roll bands. At least I don't," I admit.

"Oh, there are some fantastic women rockers out there, like Tina Turner, Joan Jett, Stevie Nicks. And the Go-Go's practically invented pop-punk. There's an all-girl grunge band called L7 that's been hitting the radio recently, too," Joan says. "We're out there. But some people don't like girl rockers up onstage. They think our voices aren't deep enough or don't have the same grit and power that men's voices do. But we're good, I know we are. The best we can do is keep at it."

"How do you get onstage when you know there are people who don't like the idea of girls in a rock band?" I ask.

"I won't lie. It's not easy," Keiko says. "Sometimes we get booed. But then I remind myself why I play, what it is I get up onstage for. I want to change their minds, but at the same time, I don't owe them anything. I'm not there to prove them wrong, although it's an added bonus. Instead, I play for myself, to say what I want to say. When I remember that, the audience melts away, and I can play my heart out."

"Yeah, those moments when people don't accept your message aren't easy. But at least we're doing something. It's better than sitting around and waiting for change. Or for someone else to do it," Joan affirms.

Although I get her point, it feels much easier—and safer—to make sure people are ready for your message than to jump ahead and risk them not hearing you. Or rejecting your idea outright.

Like what Dad is doing: holding back on sharing his idea until he gets promoted, because he doesn't want to make trouble or risk it not getting accepted.

Although Dad isn't the only one who held back when he had a risky idea. I chickened out, too, in front of Principal Klein when I wanted to ask for ESL support for Vivian.

I have a feeling Pandora's Box would have been brave enough to ask.

We arrive at Vivian's house, and Keiko pulls up the brake. The car shudders to a stop, and Vivian pushes open the door and waves goodbye as she hops out. "Bye and thank you!" she calls out.

"Don't forget that we have the homework club tomorrow after school at Power Records!" I remind her. "We did great today, but we still need those progress grades."

Vivian flashes me a thumbs-up, and as I watch her disappear inside her house, Keiko steers the car away. I direct her to my house, and a few minutes later, it comes into view. She pulls over.

"Thank you so much for today. It's been a blast," I tell them, my smile stretching wider than I think it's ever stretched.

"It was our pleasure," Keiko says. "You did great today, and you'll do great at Camp Rock Out, too."

"Don't forget, from your heart, through your chest, and out through your voice!" Joan says. The Chevy rolls down the street before disappearing into the night.

Right. Maybe I *will* end up being a great vocalist one

day . . . after I figure out what it is I want to sing about.

I head into the house and hang up my coat. Ah-ma is sitting on the couch, reading the Chinese newspaper. I shuffle my feet into slippers and join her.

"Hi, Ah-ma. How was your mahjong game today?" I greet her. "Did you make it there and back okay?" Usually, Ah-ma spends her afternoons at home, but Auntie Ying of cōng yóu bǐngs fame called yesterday and invited her to play mahjong at a local tea shop. Although it took a little convincing because Ah-ma doesn't like to leave the house without one of us with her, she agreed to go if Auntie Ying would pick her up and drop her off.

"I beat Auntie Ying twice!" Ah-ma declares, cackling. "I tell you, her cōng yóu bǐngs may be tasty, but I'm better at mahjong."

"I had no doubt you'd win." I grin.

"How did yours and Vivian's playing go today?" she asks.

"Great!" I smile proudly. "I've been practicing on my own, and it showed today. I was able to play a few chords nice and cleanly, and I feel much better about Camp Rock Out. I'm not going to show up as a total embarrassment."

"Aw, tsa-bóo-sun, that'd never happen anyway." Ah-ma squeezes my arm. The front door clicks open, and Mom walks in with Dad following close behind with bags of takeout in his hands.

"Hello, family. Look, we brought burgers home for dinner tonight." Dad puts the bags on the dining room table and takes a seat next to me on our couch. Mom heads into the kitchen, probably to get plates and utensils. "I had a late meeting today, and your mom picked me up on the way home so I didn't have to wait for the last bus. The meeting was with the hiring committee. I think I made a solid case for why I could be a strong manager for the CompuScape team. We'll see if I'll get picked for the job."

"Hooray!" I cheer. "Good for you, Dad!"

He smiles and pats down my hair like he used to do when I was little. "It's not final yet. But it's a step in the right direction."

Then he pulls back from me in a strange way. "Something looks different about you today, Lily."

I tuck my hair behind my ears, feeling shy all of a sudden. "Me? What do you mean?"

"I don't know." Dad tilts his head and inspects me closely. "You look . . . more confident. Like you've grown an inch or two taller."

"I see it, too," Mom chimes in. She puts plates on the dinner table and joins us in the living room, settling into the loveseat. "Did you do especially well on a school assignment today, Lily?"

I know what they're seeing. It's the grunge effect on their perfect, straight-A daughter.

I can't believe my transformation is already working . . . and so well that even my parents can see a difference after only a few hours of me practicing.

But should I tell them about this afternoon? They haven't been that excited about me wanting to play grunge. It's good grades that Mom and Dad care about.

It's not worth it, I decide, when Ah-ma speaks up. "What you're seeing is your daughter after playing guitar for the first time this afternoon," she says, her updo bouncing up and down in a headbang. "Like your dad used to, son."

Dad turns to me in surprise. "How?"

"Um, I know someone from the record store who plays. She invited me and Vivian to her band practice this afternoon," I confess, bracing myself for their disapproval.

He and Mom exchange a look.

"You seem pretty serious about this rock thing, Lily," Mom says. "Don't forget our agreement, though. You have to keep those grades up, okay? Vivian, too. It took quite a bit of convincing on our part to get Auntie and Uncle to agree. They still think Vivian should be doing English bǔ xí bān this summer."

I want to tell them how much I'm trying to get what they want, especially for Vivian. It's been a lot, from asking Mr. Silvers for extra time to starting the ESL Homework Club with Marcos and Yoona to even almost talking to Principal Klein about real teacher support. And I'm keeping up with my studies, too.

But I have a feeling none of it matters. If anything, they'll get upset that I've been talking to teachers. Especially Ah-ma.

"Yes, Mom," I say, holding back an eye roll. "I'll get the grades." I make up an excuse to go to my room, and when I get there, I hit Play on my stereo before flopping onto my bed. The Smashing Pumpkins' dreamy opener starts filling the room, which is perfect for how I'm feeling.

If I make it to Camp Rock Out and learn how to get up onstage and perform my heart out, will Mom and Dad care? If Camp Rock Out teaches me how to be bolder and braver, will it rub off on them, like I'm hoping it will? It looks like Dad is on his way to getting that promotion. Maybe he's right about waiting for the right moment.

Or worse, what if all my parents want is robotic, Student of the Year Lily? What if Grunge Rocker Lily means nothing to them, and they don't want that part of me around at all?

I guess I'll have plenty of sad, angry material to sing about then.

CHAPTER
18

THE NEXT DAY, WHEN VIVIAN and I get to Power Records's café for the first session of the ESL Homework Club, Yoona's already there with a few kids at a table in the middle. A boy in an olive-green beanie bustles behind the counter, taking orders from a small line of customers, and a pair of older women sip coffee in the corner.

"Hi, Yoona." I wave. "This is my cousin, Vivian."

"Nice to meet you, Vivian," Yoona says. "This is Woo-jin and Min. Woojin moved here from Seoul last year, and Min moved here six months ago from Busan."

We exchange shy hellos. Vivian and I settle into the table next to Yoona, and Yoona turns to Vivian. "What do you want to work on today? Woojin and Min are doing some grammar worksheets I photocopied at the library the other day. They wanted more practice writing."

"I would like some help with reading," Vivian says.

"Okay, why don't you try these?" Yoona slides a small stack of papers over. "They're supposed to help with reading comprehension."

I skim the worksheets. Each has a paragraph or two of text with true-or-false questions below that check what you've understood from the reading.

"Here, biǎo mèi." I pass them to Vivian. "Why don't you start working on these while I order us something? When you're done, I'll take a look."

Vivian nods and starts to read quietly to herself, her lips moving and her pencil following along each line.

I grab my wallet and get in line at the counter behind a man in a bright blue blazer and a girl in a baby-doll dress. The chalkboard menu that hangs above the register is packed full of options, from smoothies to coffee drinks to snacks to a fun array of sodas.

I'm so focused on figuring out what I want from the overwhelming menu that when someone nudges me on the shoulder, I jump with surprise.

"It's just me." Marcos grins, his eyelashes blinking innocently.

"Hey, Marcos," I reply, a bit flustered. "You made it."

Marcos points over to our group. "Yep. My cousin, Carlos, is over there with the group already."

I glance over and see a boy in a blue T-shirt and floppy hair like Marcos's—no backward green baseball cap, though—chatting with Yoona at our table. "It's nice everyone showed up. Do you think any of this will help?"

Marcos shrugs. "I dunno. But like you said the other day, it's worth a shot."

"Yeah," I reply softly. "I think it is."

"By the way, are you still planning on signing up for Camp Rock Out?"

I stare back at him, surprised. He remembered? I figured the idea of me and Vivian playing grunge was so weird that he wouldn't give it a second thought.

"Yeah, that's the plan," I say cautiously.

"Sick. That'll be a first if you two actually go. I'd pay good money to see you grunge out," he says, chuckling.

My robot defense mechanism kicks in. I'm tired of biting my tongue and people like him thinking I can't play in a rock band because of how I look.

Something in my soul pounds. I remember what Joan said last night about air coming up through your heart and out through your voice. Plus, I played electric guitar for the first time yesterday. My transformation has already started.

So I speak up. "You know, people can be more than what they seem." My voice has an edge to it that I didn't expect.

Marcos's eyebrows shoot up.

"It's like the Smashing Pumpkins." I pull out his album from my backpack and point at the cover. "Their bassist is a girl, and their lead guitarist is Japanese American. But it doesn't matter what they look like or who they are. What matters is that they love to play and that they're good at it."

As Marcos squints at the Smashing Pumpkins cover, I rummage through my backpack again. This time, I emerge with Pandora's Box's album. "There's actually an all-girl grunge band from Pacific Park that's amazing," I continue. "They're college students studying different things and are also really good rockers."

I pause for a moment, thinking. "You know, people see me and assume that the only thing I can be is the Student of the Year and do well in school. But I can play grunge if I want to. Or be the first Taiwanese American girl at Camp Rock Out."

Marcos's face softens as he inspects Pandora's Box's album. "You're right," he finally says. He stares up at the menu. "You know, I have the opposite problem from you. People might look at you and assume you're smart and that you'll always follow the rules. But people look at me and my friends and think that we're skater boys who screw around and don't care about anything or do anything right."

I remember how Principal Klein assumed right away that Marcos had done something bad that afternoon in her office, although he was actually there to translate for his aunt and uncle. I had thought the same thing when I first saw him, too, although I didn't say it out loud.

When she saw her Student of the Year, though, Principal Klein greeted me with lots of smiles and compliments.

Marcos continues. "My friends and me . . . we like to have fun, and we listen to the rules that matter. We don't accept everything as is, you know? I want to know why I should do something, instead of doing it just because someone tells me to. We aren't the screw-ups that everyone thinks we are."

I stare down at my feet. "You're right. I'm more than the Student of the Year, and you're more than a skater boy."

Our eyes meet and something clicks.

Something that feels like . . . friendship.

I don't blush this time.

The customer in front of me moves away from the counter, and it's my turn to order. I get chocolate-banana smoothies for myself and Vivian, while Marcos gets a bag of Cool Ranch Doritos and a package of Ho Hos. Then we join the table.

Vivian takes a sip of her smoothie and slides a few worksheets to me. "Okay, I've done a few. Can you take a look?"

"Of course." I skim through the first one, which is about a mailman sorting letters. I'm relieved to see that Vivian's gotten every question right.

"One hundred percent!" I scribble a big red A+ on her paper with a flourish and pass it back to her. I check the others, and she's gotten the rest of them right, too.

I knew it. She's doubting herself because she's so used to being at the top of her class. My biǎo mèi is doing fine, and she understands more than she thinks she does.

"Oh, I almost forgot!" I reach into my backpack and pull out the list of vocab words from *The Westing Game* that I had jotted down over the weekend. "I wrote down some of the harder words from our reading assignment, along with their definitions. I thought it'd be helpful to the group."

Carlos reaches for it and shakes his head. "This would have been helpful la semana pasada. But I turned in my essay yesterday, along with everyone else."

Vivian and I exchange a look. I guess Vivian was the only one who got extra time on her essay, probably because I asked Mr. Silvers for it.

I take a sip of my drink. But a small chunk of banana gets stuck in the straw and nothing comes up, no matter how hard I try.

How appropriate. What's supposed to be a nice, sweet treat to congratulate myself for getting this group of kids together isn't working out like I thought it would. Sure, everyone is heads-down and working on Yoona's worksheets, which is great. But somehow, something still doesn't feel right.

I managed to get Vivian an extra week to work on her essay, which will help her a lot. But it's not fair that Woojin, Min, and Carlos didn't get the same time to spend on theirs. Same with the other kids who Mr. Silvers had said also need some language support.

In fact, it's the kids who aren't here at ESL Homework Club who might be the worst off. They don't have family or friends like Yoona, Marcos, and me, who grew up speaking English and can help a bit.

But there's nothing I can do for them, aside from invite them to come to these sessions.

Or is there?

CHAPTER
19

THE REST OF THE WEEK is pretty event-free. We meet for our second ESL Homework Club session on Thursday, and Vivian asks about how and when to use subjective tense. Yoona, Marcos, and I do our best to explain it to everyone, but I can tell from their confused looks that we're not doing a great job.

Meanwhile, I keep practicing chords on my DIY guitar while Vivian taps out rhythms with her chopsticks-turned-drumsticks when she's not working on her essay. I add Smashing Pumpkins and Pandora's Box to my mix of grunge bands on repeat, and they go well with Pearl Jam's brooding intensity. Smashing Pumpkins is dreamy and wistful, but also hard sounding and raw like the other grunge bands. Meanwhile, every time

I listen to Pandora's Box, it fires me up with its punkish energy and powerful lyrics.

On Friday, our women's suffrage group presentation goes well, even though Logan stumbles through his section and I have to rescue him by presenting the parts he missed. Ms. King gives me extra credit for saving the project, which is nice.

Over the weekend, Vivian's still head-down working on her English lit essay and can't hang out at all. After I finish my assignments, I burn through a bunch of TV show episodes that I'd taped over the last few weeks, watching one after the other without stopping. On Sunday afternoon, I call Vivian to check in on her.

"Want me to take a look at your essay, biǎo mèi?" I ask after Uncle hands Vivian the phone.

"No," Vivian replies. "I should do it myself. Other kids don't have someone check their work before turning it in, do they?"

"I don't think so, but you're special." Plus, the stakes are high.

"Bié dān xīn, I got it, biǎo jiě," she reassures me.

On Monday, Vivian turns in her essay. When Principal Klein does her weekly broadcast over the intercom system, she reminds us that progress grades will be sent home this week. Then, during morning recess, I'm taking a sip at the drinking fountain when two kids come up to me.

"Um, you're Lily Xiao, right?" the girl with silky, straight black hair and a purple backpack asks me hesitantly. I notice that she says her Rs in an unfamiliar way, like she's rolling them around on her tongue.

"Yeah, that's me," I say, wiping my mouth with the back of my hand.

"I'm Sofia, and this is Juan." She points to the boy next to her. He's got a super short crewcut and keeps shuffling his sneakered feet back and forth. "We heard from Carlos that you are helping some kids with English after school."

Wow, word travels fast around here.

"Yeah, I'm trying, at least," I reply. "We meet on Tuesdays and Thursdays at Power Records."

"Can we join? We are both from El Salvador and some assignments are hard for us."

"Of course!" I nod. "The more the merrier." And our little ESL Homework Club grows by two more people on Tuesday.

At lunch on Thursday, when Vivian and I open Ah-ma's biàn dangs, we discover two heaping portions of má yóu jī with rice. Every bite of her warm, savory wine-stewed chicken with sesame oil makes waiting for our progress grades a little less painful.

When I get home later that day, Ah-ma calls out to me from the living room, where she's shelling a pile of peas while watching *Sān duǒ huā*.

"Some mail came for you today," she says, pointing toward the kitchen with a pod in her hand.

My heart leaps, and I drop my backpack to the ground with a thud. "Where is it?!"

"On the counter," she calls out. "There is an envelope with your name on it. But I can't read the rest."

I dash into the kitchen, and "FOR THE PARENTS OF LILY XIAO" is printed in big block letters on a big yellow envelope. The return address is listed as "Pacific Park School District."

Technically, the grades are addressed to my parents, but it's got my name on it, so it's probably okay for me to open. Hands trembling, I grab the letter opener from the kitchen drawer and slide it down the edge of the envelope. Then I pull out the papers inside.

The first thing I see is some letter to the parents from Principal Klein, thanking them for entrusting Pacific Park Middle with the future of their children . . . blah blah blah.

I find the real stuff. The chart that outlines my progress for the term is printed in purple block letters on a thin white piece of paper. My classes are listed in the first column, and the grades for this quarter are in the second . . .

And it's all As.

"Woo-hoo!!" I scream.

Lily Xiao delivers again.

But this time, I didn't just make my parents happy. I also managed to get something I want—registration for Camp Rock Out!

Ah-ma rushes into the kitchen like a flying rooster, her eyes frantic. "What's going on, Lily?" Pea pods drop from her hands to the floor as she reaches for the letter. "What is this about?"

"Ah-ma, it's my progress grades! I did great, which means I get to go to Camp Rock Out this summer!"

"Oh, my goodness, I thought something bad had happened." Ah-ma puts her hand over her heart, like she's trying to slow it down.

"Sorry to scare you, Ah-ma!" I pat her arm reassuringly. "But this is so, so, so awesome." I give Ah-ma a big hug. "I'm going to learn guitar like Ah-gong! I have to go call Vivian. We're going to be in a band together!"

I dash down the hallway, grab the phone, and pull it into my room. I flop down on my beanbag chair and dial my future drummer's number.

The phone rings a few times before Auntie's voice crackles into the receiver. "Wéi?"

"Nǐ hǎo, Auntie," I greet my aunt, my breath quick with excitement. "Can I talk to Vivian? I've got some news to share with her!"

There's a long pause on the phone, which is kind of weird. Auntie is usually super quick to hand the phone over.

"Hello?" I say again.

Auntie finally speaks. "I'm sorry, Lily, but Vivian can't come to the phone right now. Can she call you back later?"

"Um, sure," I fumble in response. "Is everything okay?"

"We're sorting some things out. She'll call you later."

Click. Auntie hangs up without saying goodbye.

Uh-oh. Something's not right.

There's no way Vivian didn't do well enough on her progress grades, though. With all her studying, plus my help and the ESL Homework Club—her grades must have improved this semester.

I'm sure it's nothing.

After I go back to the kitchen and help Ah-ma pick the peas up off the floor, I settle onto the couch. I'm two songs into a repeat showing of Pearl Jam's Unplugged performance on MTV when the phone rings.

"Hey, biǎo jiě. Sorry it took so long for me to call you back." Vivian's voice is unusually quiet, even a bit gravelly.

"It's okay," I reply, relieved to finally have my drummer on the phone. "My progress grades came in today!"

There's a beat of silence. "How did you do?"

"Woo-hoo!" I hoot. "Straight As across the board for me. And you know what that means . . ." I pause for dramatic effect. "I can go to Camp Rock Out!" I seriously think my heart is about to burst. Both me and Vivian, up onstage, rocking our hearts out to music like Pearl Jam or Pandora's Box? "Oh my gosh, we're going to have the best time, biǎo mèi!"

It's a dream come true.

"But wait, Lily . . . there's a problem," Vivian says quietly.

A problem?

Vivian continues. "My grades came in today, too."

Then it dawns on me. "Wait . . . and how are they?"

"Lily, I got a very bad mark in English literature."

"What?!"

"Mr. Silvers said he had a hard time following my midterm paper. He called my parents this afternoon and said that he had to give me a C- on my progress report. Which means . . ."

My heart pounds in my ears.

". . . you can't go to Camp Rock Out." I finish Vivian's sentence.

No Vivian means no camp for me, either. We spend every summer together, no matter what. And there's no way I'm getting up on that stage by myself.

A lump the size of a bah-oân rises in my throat and I try to breathe through my nose.

Vivian bursts into sobs. "Oh, biǎo jiě, I'm so sorry. I thought that if I worked hard enough and did enough of those worksheets, I'd be able to catch up. But I couldn't."

"What about the ESL Homework Club? Didn't that help?"

"I guess it wasn't enough," she sniffs.

My heart breaks, and guilt starts to flood in. I've failed in my duty to watch out for my biǎo mèi. I'm still confused about how this could have happened, though. Maybe Mr. Silvers was too harsh for some reason. If he was, maybe I can go back and argue for a grade change. "Can you read me the first paragraph of your essay, Vivian?"

"Lily, it's too late. The grade is in. What's the point?" Frustration spills from her voice.

"I know, biǎo mèi," I say softly. "But maybe I can talk to Mr. Silvers again. He knows how hard this is for you. I can fix this. I know I can."

"Fine. Hold on." Shuffling noises come through from Vivian's side of the phone. "Here's how it starts . . ." Vivian reads the first paragraph of her paper out loud in her slow English.

As I listen, my heart sinks. It *is* hard to follow what Vivian's trying to say. She's flipped the order of the subject and verb in a lot of sentences, and she uses the singular instead of the plural with a bunch of nouns. Her pronouns are also mixed up.

Vivian finishes. "Well?"

I bite my lower lip, thinking. "Can you read it one more time? Slower?"

As she reads, I try to translate what she's saying in English into Chinese. When I do that, what she's saying makes a lot more sense.

In fact, it's insightful. She understands the complicated story and has picked up on the themes of capitalism and prejudice and solidarity. This can only mean one thing.

"Vivian, this isn't your fault. It's about writing in English, isn't it?"

"Yeah," Vivian practically whispers.

I knew it. It's about her thoughts getting lost in translation, not about how well she understood the book.

Which meant she knew this might happen.

Vivian's been saying for weeks now that following the complicated plot of *The Westing Game* has been super hard for her. That's why we've been working on learning vocab and doing worksheets focused on reading comprehension. But she hadn't said a word about also needing help with grammar rules or writing practice.

Why didn't Vivian work on those things, too?

On top of that, my own biǎo mèi didn't trust me enough to tell me the truth about how she was really doing, even after all I'd done for her.

Like ask a teacher for a favor.

Like try to confront a principal.

Like start an ESL Homework Club with a bunch of kids I barely knew.

I even offered to proofread her essay, and she said no.

And now I can't go to Camp Rock Out.

My guilt turns into the beginnings of anger and frustration. "Vivian. Why didn't you let me proofread your essay? I would have caught these errors," I accuse her.

"I thought I could do it on my own. And letting you see my essay would have been cheating," Vivian replies slowly.

"I didn't want you to cheat. I wanted to help. You knew what was on the line here! You knew how important it was to get this right!"

"Hey, you were the one who promised our parents that we'd get good grades before checking in with me first," Vivian snaps back. "You were the one who made our grades a condition for going to Camp Rock Out."

My stomach churns in that weird way it did when I made that deal a few weeks ago. I can't deny that my decision did create more pressure for Vivian. I probably should have discussed the idea with her.

Still, she hasn't been honest with me. And that hurts, too.

I take a deep breath and try to shift the focus of this

conversation back onto her. "I made the deal because I didn't know how badly you were doing. You always did fine back in Taiwan. Plus, I thought it was only the reading that was hard for you. At least that's what you told me."

"I thought I could do the rest." Vivian's voice turns from defensive to desperate. "And you're right. Back in Taipei, I'd always been able to figure out this kind of stuff. I was sure I could do it this time, too."

"Well, obviously you couldn't, and now there's no Camp Rock Out. I'm stuck being the way I am—perfectly boring."

Vivian takes in a short breath from the other side of the phone . . .

And attacks back. "You think school is so easy for everyone else because it's easy for you?" Vivian yells. "Well, it's not! And I know the truth, Lily."

I stare at the receiver with big, surprised eyes. Vivian's never ever yelled at me like this before.

Then again, I've never yelled at my biǎo mèi, either. But I've also never wanted something so badly.

"What truth?" I growl back. "You mean the truth that you hid from me?"

"No. The truth that you're only helping me because Ah-ma asked you to. You were doing it to make her happy. Not because you care about me. You're being selfish and only helping me to get what you want."

My mouth drops open.

She's not done, though. "And what you want is Camp Rock Out. It's been your idea all along. But have you ever stopped to think about what I want? Or more importantly, what I need?"

By now, my stomach isn't just churning anymore. It's in full spin-cycle mode, like my insides are laundry being tossed around the belly of a washing machine.

I'm about to be sick.

I don't get it. What is Vivian talking about? Doesn't she want Camp Rock Out, too?

Like a flood breaking open a dam, Vivian's frustration keeps spilling out, overwhelming me and my confused brain. "Besides, what's this about you being stuck the way you are? What's wrong with who you are? Why do you care so much about what other people think? The more you care, the more scared you become. Maybe you *are* a chicken."

Then Vivian hangs up with a clank.

Now that's one way to end a rock song: with a loud, passionate bang from the percussionist.

I stare at the phone in my hand, the sharp, insistent dial tone piercing the air around me. My mind whirls with the harsh words Vivian and I just flung at each other, like barbed arrows hitting tender, weak targets in the flurry of battle.

What on earth just happened? How did this afternoon

go from me finally getting to go to Camp Rock Out to an all-out phone fight with my biǎo mèi? How did it go from the promise of a shiny new me to the accusation that I'm a selfish, awful, cowardly chicken? And from the one person who's supposed to know me the best?

Robot: abort. Abort. Abort transformation mode.

CHAPTER
20

WHEN I SIT DOWN AT the dinner table later that night, I see that Ah-ma's made stuffed bitter melon along with steamed fish and our usual white rice. Usually, the bumpy, pale green vegetable is one of my favorites—crunchy like a cucumber with a sharp yet refreshing taste.

But tonight, I don't have an appetite.

I'm already bitter about Camp Rock Out. And my fight with Vivian.

After listening to Pearl Jam's loudest songs for an hour on repeat, though, the edges of my anger don't feel as sharp as they were.

Instead, they've been dulled down by guilt, disappointment, and sadness churning away in my stomach.

All I've done hasn't been enough to help Vivian, she's not going to get to go to Camp Rock Out, and the sad truth is . . . she's totally right about me.

I *am* scared, selfish, and a chicken. Pretty much everything that's the opposite of grunge.

The thing is, that's exactly why I need to go to Camp Rock Out. It's why I need to learn how to be someone else.

But that's not going to happen now. Not without Vivian.

After Mom comes in from the kitchen, she doesn't take a seat right away. Instead, she stays on her feet and holds up her teacup. "Lily, Ah-ma told us about your progress grades. Congratulations, gong xǐ, gong xǐ! You've fulfilled your end of the deal, and Dad and I are going to send in your registration forms for that rock-and-roll summer camp tomorrow." She beams at me. . . .

And I burst into tears. *Robot malfunction. Alert. Alert.*

"Lily! What happened?" Mom rushes to my side and rubs my back as a cascade of sobs floods over me. Dad reaches across the table and places his hand on my arm, squeezing it with concern.

Everything comes out in a blubbering mess—Vivian's bad grade, me not wanting to go to Camp Rock Out without her, and the horrible things we said to each other.

"Oh no," Mom breathes out. "I'm so sorry to hear

about Vivian's lack of progress. She's been working so hard."

Of course the one thing Mom takes away from my breakdown is how Vivian's doing in school. Not that I've failed as a biǎo jiě and lost the chance to finally turn into someone better than my shy, awkward self.

"Haven't you been helping her, Lily?" Ah-ma asks.

"Yes," I sniff. "I've been working with her on the English translations of the book. I talked to Mr. Silvers to get her extra time for her homework. . . . I even offered to proofread her essay. But none of it worked."

Ah-ma's chopsticks pause in midair. "You spoke to your teacher about getting Vivian extra help? But that's disrespectful to his teaching methods!"

"Ah-ma, I was very polite when I asked, and he didn't get upset or annoyed," I reply as patiently as I can. "He can't help much, anyway. He says if we really want Vivian to get some professional tutoring, we have to talk to Principal Klein and ask her to request funding for ESL classes from the district."

"There's no need for us to do that." Ah-ma shakes her head. "We must be resourceful and think of other ways to get Vivian to where she needs to be."

"I have been! I've even been getting together with a group of other kids who have family and friends who need English help. We've been trying to tutor them together," I say, wiping my nose with the back of my hand. "Clearly it's not enough, though."

"Xiān kǔ hòu tián." Ah-ma points her chopsticks at the plate of bitter melon and hands me a tissue. "Sometimes you have to eat bitter before you can taste sweet. Vivian can do it. But it takes time."

"Ma's right. Learning anything new takes hard work. I know how disappointed you are that Vivian won't be going to this camp with you. But you could still go," Dad suggests gently.

"I don't want to go by myself," I say forcefully. "And I can't leave her alone this summer."

Dad shakes his head. "If Vivian's struggling that much with English, it is probably better for her to do English bǔ xí bān this summer instead of this music camp."

"No," I insist. "Vivian has to do it with me."

"Why?"

"Dad, we're family. We have to be together." I can't believe my parents don't get how important it is for me and Vivian to do this, side by side. She's going to be an amazing drummer, and we'd make such a powerful grunge-rock duo. Plus, I can't ditch her for four whole weeks. She has no one else to hang out with here in Pacific Park.

Me neither, actually. But with her bubbly personality to help break the ice with all those kids who love the same music as we do, we'll make new friends for sure.

Although I still don't get what she meant earlier about what she wants and needs. She wants to go to Camp Rock Out . . . doesn't she?

"How much time do you and Vivian have before you have to sign up for this camp?" Dad asks.

I sniff. "Two weeks."

He taps his chopsticks against his rice bowl. "I see how hard Vivian's been trying, and I'd love to see her enjoy some summer activities. How about I talk to Auntie and see if we can figure out another way to get Vivian some more help? Then they may let Vivian go to your camp."

"What other way?" I ask skeptically.

"Maybe she can come over and I tutor her? I had to learn English, too, so I know what she should look out for. Between the three of us, I'm sure we can make a difference."

I bite my lip, thinking hard. Dad speaks English well, but it's not perfect. She deserves help from someone who knows how to teach ESL students.

In other words, a real teacher with real credentials.

Something about this whole situation doesn't feel . . . What's the word I'm looking for?

Fair. This isn't fair.

Sure, maybe I could have done more. And maybe Vivian could have asked for help earlier.

But at the same time, she's done the best she can. Maybe we need to take this to someone with the power to do something about it.

Someone who can help more kids than Vivian. Dad and I can tutor our flesh and blood, but we can't possibly tutor Carlos, Woojin, Min, and all the other ESL kids at Pacific Park Middle, too.

"You tutoring her would be nice, Dad," I reply carefully. "But you've got so much going on already. Mr. Silvers said that Pacific Park Middle used to offer ESL programs taught by real teachers. Maybe you could talk to Principal Klein and ask if she can start them up again."

"Talk to the principal? No, we can't do that," Ah-ma interjects.

"Why not? Other parents ask for what their kids need all the time. And it's not only Vivian who needs ESL help. I know at least five other kids who could use some focused tutoring."

Ah-ma shakes her head, her hair wobbling up high. "Absolutely not. We can't go to authorities like that and question their approach. It can only lead to bad things."

"Like what? What if their approach isn't right?"

Dad puts his hand on mine, eyebrows furrowed behind his black-rimmed glasses. "Lily, we feel lucky that we're here in the US at all. The US government doesn't give visas to just anybody. Your mom and I got lucky fourteen years ago. Now that we're here, our whole family should be grateful for the opportunity, which means we don't ask for more. We make do with what's been given to us."

"But, Dad," I protest, "what if what they're giving us isn't enough? Shouldn't we all get a fair chance to learn what we need to?"

"Lily, I know how much you want to go to this camp and how much you want Vivian to be with you. But things will work out. The school knows what they're doing with students like her. Sometimes you have to let things take their course. I'll talk to Auntie about other solutions we can figure out on our own."

"But, Dad . . ."

"Lily, it's a no. We will not speak to your principal about this." Dad's voice is hard and firm.

I close my mouth and stab a piece of bitter melon instead. "Fine. You handle it."

But what's in my heart is more bitter than what I'm tasting right now.

Camp Rock Out wasn't only going to teach me how to be loud and defiant. It was also going to help my family see that they could stand up and speak out, too, that it was okay to do things like play loud music or argue with a school principal to ask for what a family member needs.

Instead, they're not doing anything, and I'm supposed to shut my mouth and let other people take care of my problems.

I'm getting real sick of it.

After dinner is over and I escape back to my room, I curl up with the fluffy pink blanket on my bed.

It's wallowing-in-self-pity time.

My eyes wander restlessly around my room. They take in my Xiǎo Dīng Dāng collection, and tears come to my eyes as I think about how that robot cat is always there to help Nobito, no matter what.

As for me? I couldn't deliver in the same way.

My gaze lands on the Pearl Jam poster taped up above my desk. It's a black-and-white shot of Eddie Vedder, alone and in profile as he sings at a concert in Seattle. His face is twisted and intense as he shouts into the mic in front of a crowd with their fists in the air. I love this poster because it's a simple shot that shows a ton of emotion and feeling. Eddie's no robot. No one is telling him what to sing about. Or how to sing.

This can't be over. There's got to be another way to get me and Vivian to Camp Rock Out.

Vivian has tried so hard, and I assumed that her effort was going to pay off. What you put in is what you get out, right?

But in Vivian's case, hard work hasn't been enough.

There are barriers in her way that she can't clear herself. Even with the help of Pacific Park Middle's Student of the Year.

I stare at my guitar, and Joan's words about why she plays grunge rock echo in my head. *At least we're doing something. It's better than sitting around and waiting for something to change. Or for someone else to do it.*

I need to stop being a chicken.

I need to change things myself.

The way to do that is to talk to Principal Klein myself about ESL classes at Pacific Park Middle. What's the harm? If she says no, my family will never know what I've done.

But it's worth a try. If she says yes, then I would have done a good thing. I'd be helping the other kids in ESL Homework Club, too, not to mention those at Pacific Park Middle who don't come to our sessions and need the language support.

Yes, talking to Principal Klein is what Eddie would do. I can be grateful that my family's here, in a place with lots of opportunity. But at the same time, I can be strong and ask for what my family needs.

Or more accurately, what they deserve.

I'll talk to Principal Klein tomorrow. She'll fix this.

CHAPTER
21

WHEN THE END-OF-SCHOOL BELL RINGS, I head straight to Principal Klein's office. When I open the door that leads to the waiting room, Ms. Jensen, her assistant, greets me right away.

"Ah, it's Lily! Are you here to meet with Principal Klein about something?" she asks from behind the counter, her gold bracelets clanking together as she types on a computer.

I nod shyly.

"Well, she's free right now, so go on in."

I take a deep breath, march over to the office door, and open it quickly. I don't want to give myself time today to back out.

Not like two weeks ago.

Unlike the eggshell-yellow walls of the waiting room, Principal Klein's office is a dark forest green. A big wooden table squats in the middle, its smooth surface covered in neat stacks of paper. Behind the table are shelves of official-looking leatherbound books, sprinkled with a few placards and trophies in between. From where I'm standing, I can see the text on the biggest one, which reads "Principal Achievement Award for Outstanding Leadership 1990."

Principal Klein sits behind the desk in a black leather chair that squeaks as she twists it in my direction. In front of the table are two wooden chairs with brick-red cushions.

"Ah, Lily, my Student of the Year. Please sit." She motions for me to take a seat. I slip off my backpack and hook it behind a chair before settling in, my heart pounding. The fabric is rough and scratchy, forcing me to sit up straight, rather than sink comfortably into it.

Principal Klein folds her hands in front of her on the desk and looks at me with her piercing blue eyes. "I didn't expect to see you here. What can I do for you?"

I do my best to ignore how nervous and guilty I feel about disobeying my parents, not to mention Ah-ma. Instead, I try to channel the grit and guts of the Pearl Jam music I so desperately want to play.

"My cousin, Vivian, is having a hard time with

school," I begin. "She's super smart, but English isn't her first language. She did study it in school back in Taipei, but it's not good enough that she can keep up in more advanced classes, like English literature."

Principal Klein adjusts a pen that's lying on her desk to line up perfectly with the edge. "Moving countries and having to adopt a new language isn't easy."

"It isn't," I say. "I was thinking . . . could the school give her some help, like specialized tutoring for English? Mr. Silvers told me that Pacific Park Middle used to offer ESL classes. Could you do that again?" I give Principal Klein my best "please, please, pretty please" face, although I try to mix in as much politeness and respect as I can.

Principal Klein looks at me carefully. "Let me ask you a question, Lily. Did Vivian and her family move here by choice?"

I stare back at her.

"Uh, what do you mean, Principal Klein?" And what does that have to do with anything?

"What I mean is . . . did they want to come here? They weren't sent here for any particular reason, were they?"

"Um, no, they moved here because they wanted to be close to my family. And to my grandma. My dad and Vivian's mom are brother and sister, and my grandma lives with us."

"I see," Principal Klein replies. "They came for personal reasons, right?"

I nod.

"I ask because it's important to remember that they chose to come here. In doing so, they made a choice to adopt American culture, which means they need to get used to the way we do things here."

I'm not sure where Principal Klein is going. But I listen patiently, like a good student should.

"Hearing English and speaking it every day is one of the most important ways immigrant children will start to understand American culture," she says. "For that reason, full English immersion is best."

"What does full immersion mean?" I ask.

"It means the person is completely integrated in an English-only environment. They listen to English, they speak in English, they read in English. That way, they learn much faster."

"Vivian's trying hard to absorb it all," I say. "But it doesn't seem to be working."

"She'll get there. It sounds like she has a big family here," Principal Klein observes. "What language do you speak when you're together?"

"We speak in Mandarin Chinese and Taiwanese," I reply proudly.

Principal Klein crosses her arms and leans back in

her chair. "That's one of the problems. That's not full immersion, is it? Your cousin will never get better at English if she's still relying on Chinese when she's not at school."

"But Vivian's parents don't speak English very well, either. My grandma can't speak it at all."

"Sounds like your family has their work cut out for them." Principal Klein watches as I squirm in my seat.

What Principal Klein expects when it comes to speaking English at home doesn't seem very realistic. How are we supposed to enjoy each other if we can't tell each other how we're feeling?

Plus, language is one of our strongest links back to Taiwan.

"Chinese is really, really different from English, though. It doesn't even use the same alphabet. Our grammar structure is totally different, and we don't have tenses or pronouns." I try to explain why what she's suggesting is practically impossible. "Please, isn't there anything the school can do to help her learn better? Even something like after-school tutoring?"

Principal Klein shakes her head. "She can do it through immersion like she's doing now. She's a smart cookie. You all are."

"We all are?" I ask, tilting my head in confusion.

"You know, kids like you. Or that other student . . . Yoona. From Asia."

"Asia is a big continent," I say, trying to hold back the impatience rising to the surface. "My family is from Taiwan, and Yoona's is from South Korea," I point out. "They're totally different countries with different languages and customs. And I was born here in Pacific Park." My ears start to get tingly.

Principal Klein waves her hand in the air, like what I said didn't make a difference. "The point is you come from well-educated families. If you help each other, English will come."

My stomach churns at her words. How can she assume that Vivian, or me for that matter, are from a "well-educated family"? In our case, it's true that our parents graduated from college back in Taiwan. But it's not the case for every Chinese or Taiwanese person in Pacific Park.

Or any kid who needs help with English.

Plus, even though my parents went to college, they spend their energy working hard at their jobs, like my dad trying to get computers to connect so they can exchange information with each other, or my mom who makes sure businesses stay running. Their English is good enough—but their sights are set on something bigger than perfecting language.

Plus, Yoona and I *are* helping each other with the ESL Homework Club. Marcos, too. Or at least we're trying to. But it wasn't enough for Vivian.

What Principal Klein is saying is wrong, and I push myself to say it.

"But Principal Klein, you can't assume that every kid from Asia comes from an educated family. What about kids whose parents don't have time to study with them because they're too busy working? Or whose parents *are* educated but don't speak English at all?"

Principal Klein leans back in her chair again. "Lily, I'll say it again—full immersion is the way to go. We're a public school, not a private one like Evergreen Prep. We don't have the money to give a small group of students specialized bilingual education, not to mention finding educators who can speak the different languages we'd need. In California, there are too many languages we'd need to support. Chinese, Korean, Spanish, Tagalog, Vietnamese—we can't do it. We can't offer instruction in both English and all those other languages."

"It wouldn't be a small group, though. A bunch of us get together now to tutor English, and there are plenty of kids who show up at our sessions. Even though they speak different languages at home, some of the things they need help with are the same. One class could help them at once." My voice is getting higher, and I can feel that *thump thump* of my heart. I'm starting to get angry.

"Lily, I understand that you're frustrated. But we don't have the funds at Pacific Park Middle to offer those classes. I do believe that the more exposure your cousin has, the faster she will learn. It takes time."

But we don't have time. Camp Rock Out registration forms are due in two weeks. Something needs to change . . . and fast.

Then Ah-ma's voice starts echoing in my head. *Keep your head down. Don't make trouble.*

If I don't say anything, though, I'm not going to get what I want. And what I want is Camp Rock Out.

So for the first time ever, I try to listen to what *my* inner voice is telling me to do. "Principal Klein, couldn't you ask the district for the funding? Mr. Silvers says that the principal of the school can request it if it's what the students need," I suggest, trying to speak as firmly as I can.

Principal Klein's lips press together, and she clasps her hands in front of her on the table again. "Lily, it's a no. If kids can't handle the work, we keep them back for a year. It's only a year, and if they work really hard, they'll catch up." Her voice is stern with a touch of what sounds like anger.

My breath catches in my throat. Did I make Principal Klein mad? I didn't mean to take it that far.

Ah-ma's words echo in my head again: *Don't cause any trouble, Lily.*

But that fire is still burning in me. This isn't right. I can't believe Principal Klein won't help.

I owe it one more try.

"Principal Klein, I'm the Student of the Year. What if you got someone to train me? Or other volunteer students, like Yoona and Marcos. If the school can't do it, maybe the students can. But we don't know how."

Principal Klein's eyebrows shoot up. "Marcos Alvarez?"

I straighten my shoulders. "Yes. He's trying to help his cousin."

Principal Klein lets out a slow breath and takes off her glasses.

"I didn't expect you of all people, Lily, to be so . . . stubborn. You're free to help these students in any way you can. But the school doesn't have more resources. We're tight enough already."

I can tell from the expression on her face that Principal Klein isn't going to budge. The only thing I can do now is swallow down my annoyance and force myself to thank her for her time.

As I head out of her office, she speaks again. "Wait, Lily. One more thing . . ."

I spin around, hope springing to my chest.

Principal Klein takes a stack of papers from a pile on her desk and hands them to me. "Work through these with your cousin. They'll help, I promise."

I take them from her. They're the same worksheets that Yoona had given Woojin, Min, Carlos, and Vivian.

This is the best the principal of Pacific Park Middle School can do? Seriously?

I mumble a thank-you and goodbye and book it out of there before the pent-up anger boiling in my body explodes.

So much for being Student of the Year. I didn't get a single thing I wanted.

Or that my cousin needs.

CHAPTER
22

"I NEED TO TALK TO Vivian, Auntie. Please?" It's Saturday morning, and I'm standing at the front door of Vivian's house. I owe her a huge apology for what a jerk I've been.

Auntie's looking at me with a stern expression on her face. "Lily, Vivian can't be distracted anymore. We need to make sure she gets back on track," she says, shaking her head.

"I know." I stare down at my Doc Martens. "But I said some mean things to her, and I need to make it right." Tears spring to my eyes.

Auntie hesitates, then gives in. "Okay. I'll bring her out."

A few minutes later, Vivian joins me on the front

steps. She's in baggy sweatpants and a white T-shirt, nothing like the cheerful, colorful self she usually is.

Her face isn't angry, though. It's just plain sad.

I grab her hand. My apology comes rushing out in a flood of words. "Biǎo mèi, I'm so, so, so sorry. I said horrible things that I shouldn't have. You haven't let me down, and I shouldn't have blamed you for not doing well. You're right. I've been selfish. None of this is your fault."

Vivian's eyes fill with tears. "I really thought I could write the essay on my own."

I shake my head. "There are problems in your way that you couldn't solve by yourself, Vivian." I think of the awful conversation I had with Principal Klein yesterday. "I can't solve them, either," I add softly.

Vivian plops down on the front steps and hugs her knees. I join her and put my arm around her shoulders.

"It's hard for me to admit I need help," she mutters, avoiding my eyes. "I think it's hard for Mom and Dad, too. We're used to thinking that if you work hard enough, you'll get what you want." She rests her chin on her knees and stares into the distance.

"Yeah, that's what I thought, too," I admit. "But obviously, that's not true, because you tried so hard. Dad said he'd talk to your parents about another way to get some help, though. It's not over yet," I say, trying to sound hopeful. "There's still a chance we can make it to Camp Rock Out."

Vivian shifts her weight around, then clears her throat. "Things are worse than us not going to camp together, biǎo jiě."

I stare at her. "What do you mean?"

Her eyes get watery again. "I overheard my parents last night talking about how they think I should transfer schools to Evergreen Prep. Because of the extra help I'd get at a private school."

What?! My heart drops. "We won't go to the same school anymore?"

She shakes her head.

"But how would your parents pay for it? If they can't afford a tutor for you now, how are they going to afford private school tuition?"

"Ah-ma will help. Your family, too . . . Something about bringing family money from Taiwan to here. But it's going to be tight. Going to Evergreen means we'll need to start saving money and cutting expenses. My mom was saying how we might have to move to a different apartment, smaller and farther away, but cheaper."

I can't believe what Vivian's telling me. This is my family's plan to help? It's not what I had in mind at all!

"Is this definitely going to happen?" I ask desperately.

Vivian hugs her knees closer to her chest. "Once Mom and Dad figure out the money part, yes. I heard them say something about paying the first semester tuition by the end of April."

My mind whirls. There's got to be a way to stop this from happening.

"That's a few weeks away. We can still try to get Pacific Park Middle to offer ESL classes, like the ones public schools used to have and Evergreen has now. Then you'll be getting help at Pacific Park Middle next year and won't have to go to Evergreen. It's not too late."

"But how are you going to convince the school to offer ESL classes?" Vivian sounds totally defeated.

I stand up straight. "I don't know. I'll figure something out, though." Maybe there's another way to get through to Principal Klein—one that can't be ignored. I have to try again.

I can't lose my best friend.

When I get home, Dad's at the dining table helping Ah-ma make more bah-oân, while Mom's in the living room folding laundry.

"Ah, tsa-bóo-sun! Welcome home. Will you come help me and chat?" Ah-ma pats the seat next to her, beaming as usual, like everything's normal.

But I know the truth. I know what they're plotting behind my back.

"Sorry, Ah-ma, but I've got a lot of homework today," I grumble before retreating to my room.

I can't believe that my whole family is in on Auntie

and Uncle's plans. It's like they're trying to pull me and Vivian apart. What's worse is that they haven't said a word to me about it. It looks like my family decided to do things their way, too, without asking me for my opinion.

Now it's time for me to take things into my own hands and do things my way. . . .

For once.

CHAPTER
23

"WHAT'S THE BIG EMERGENCY, LILY?" Marcos asks as he lazily tosses his baseball cap up and down in his hands. "Why'd you call us to meet you at the library on a Sunday morning?"

Yoona peers back at me curiously. "Yeah, what's going on?" she asks, tucking a black curl behind her right ear.

"Before I tell you, do you two know how Carlos, Woojin, and Min did on their progress grades?" I ask.

Marcos runs his fingers through his hair. "Same as usual, unfortunately. No real improvement."

Yoona shrugs. "I don't know for sure with Woojin and Min. But if they did better, their parents would have called mine to tell us."

"Yeah, I thought that the ESL Homework Club would

be enough to help Vivian do better on her progress grades. But it wasn't," I say. "Even with our help and an extra week to work on her essay, she still didn't get a good grade in English lit." I take a deep breath. "Enough is enough. I think we need to do more to convince the school to offer ESL classes."

"You do? How?" Yoona leans forward in her chair.

"What Principal Klein is expecting these kids—and us—to do isn't fair. Our friends and family are at a disadvantage because of language, and they'll get further and further behind, even if they work super hard. I tried to talk to Principal Klein, and she doesn't want to change things. But I think she's wrong. And we can make her see it."

"How would we do that?" Marcos wonders out loud.

I take a deep breath and launch into the plan I came up with last night. "We could start a petition, like the suffragettes did in the 1920s. We could gather signatures from kids and parents who support ESL classes at Pacific Park Middle. It'd show that there's real demand from a lot of students. I mean, if petitioning worked for the original girl grunge rockers of American history, then it could work for us, too."

"A petition?" Marcos sits up straight in his seat. "You think there are enough people who'd sign it?"

"We won't know unless we try," I assert.

"Wait, what kind of ESL class are we asking for, though?" Yoona asks. "Would these classes be taught in English? Or would there be one taught in Spanish for the Spanish-speaking kids, then one in Korean for the Korean kids, and so on?" She looks worried. "That seems complicated."

I think for a minute. "Honestly, I don't know what would work at Pacific Park Middle. It'd probably depend on how many ESL students there are and what languages they speak. But the school should be able to figure that out. All we're asking for is that they explore different solutions, then pick the one that works for the most students."

Marcos pushes his baseball cap lower on his head. "That makes sense. We're not telling the school what to do. We just want Principal Klein to try something besides English immersion."

Yoona pushes her round glasses up her nose. "Why the sudden urgency? I mean, I totally think classes taught by real teachers is the way to go. But why now?"

I open my mouth to explain Camp Rock Out and the registration date that is fast approaching. And the tuition deposit for Evergreen Prep.

Then I close it.

Camp Rock Out isn't the only reason anymore. I still want to go, and with Vivian. But what's most important is getting my biǎo mèi the help she needs. And it has to be here at Pacific Park Middle, not at some outrageously expensive private school that's going to force her to leave our school and her family to move across town.

I pull my shoulders back and jut my chin. "Because I care about my cousin. Because she's family. And I don't want to wait for change anymore."

"Dude, that's sick." Marcos reaches his hands behind his head and leans back in his chair, balancing it on its back legs. "I get it."

I smile back at him. "Yeah, helping your family is pretty . . . sick."

Yoona and Marcos burst out laughing. For a second, I'm horrified—did I just embarrass myself with my ridiculous attempt to sound cool?

But when I see Yoona and Marcos giggle, I can't help but join in, too.

It feels good to laugh with other kids.

"Seriously, what do you guys think?" I put on my best begging face.

Yoona and Marcos exchange glances. Then Marcos tilts the chair he's been tottering on forward, and the front legs hit the ground with a bang. "I'm in. Let's shake things up."

Yoona grins. "Okay, I'm in, too."

Whew.

I don't have a real rock band yet—that's not going to happen until I make it to Camp Rock Out.

But this may be the next best thing.

We spend the afternoon working on our petition's mission statement. After a bunch of drafts, we finally agree on one that we're happy with. I carefully copy the text down on a clean sheet of paper, making sure to leave plenty of space on the bottom for lines where people can sign their names.

"Here." I finish the last line with a flourish. "All done!"

Marcos reads the petition out loud:

Petition for School-Funded ESL Classes

We, the students, parents, and guardians of Pacific Park Middle School, are petitioning the leaders to provide English-as-a-Second-Language support for any kid who needs it. Right now, lots of students can't keep up because their native languages are not English, and they do not have help at home or the money to pay for it. We believe that it is the school's responsibility to provide every student with a fair chance at a good education, no matter where they are from or what language they speak.

All of us below support school-funded ESL classes:

Name	Student or Guardian	Phone Number	Signature

"This looks great," Yoona says proudly.

But something doesn't feel quite right. "Wait, what if there are parents who can't read English? We need to make sure they understand what they're signing," I say.

Marcos chews on the rubber end of his pencil. "We'll have to make versions of the petition in different languages. I can write the Spanish one."

"I'll write one in Korean," Yoona adds. "Lily, could you do the Chinese one?"

I hesitate for a moment. My written Chinese isn't nearly as good as my spoken Chinese. If I were brave enough, I'd ask Dad or Ah-ma to help me.

But there's no way they'd be okay with what I'm about to do.

"My written Chinese isn't perfect," I reply slowly. "But I can write well enough to get the gist across. I think. And my cousin can check it."

Yoona taps her pen against the table. "We can ask other kids, too. . . . Like Trinh Nguyen for one in

Vietnamese, or Alex Ocampo to do one in Tagalog."

"Perfect!" I exclaim. I just hope we'll be able to do it fast enough. Time is ticking on Vivian's school transfer. And on those Camp Rock Out registration forms.

We spend the next few minutes rewriting the petitions in our other languages. Then we empty our pockets for coins and head to the copy machine.

"Now we need to figure out how we're going to get signatures and how quickly we want to do this," I say as the machine hums and spits out copies of our petition.

"We want Principal Klein to take this to the school board, right?" Yoona says.

I nod. "Yes, she needs to ask the district for money to pay for the ESL programs."

"Anyone know when the next board meeting is?" Marcos asks.

"I have no idea. But we're in a library." I sweep my arms in a big circle. "The answer's got to be in here somewhere."

I lead Marcos and Yoona to the information desk, where a librarian is sorting library cards. We ask him if he can help us figure out when the next school board meeting is, and he takes us to the newspaper and magazine section. He stops in front of a shelf that's got wooden rods stretching across the width at different heights. Draped around each one are newspapers, their pages hanging like clothes on a drying line.

The librarian pulls a wooden bar off the rack and turns it ninety degrees so that the newspaper is upright and we can read the words properly. "This is the latest issue of the *Pacific Park Weekly*." Flipping through, he turns to a section that reads "Education."

The three of us peek over his shoulder. There's an article about a high school football game, a profile on a librarian's campaign for more diverse books, and a feature on a theater performance by one of the elementary schools.

It's fun stuff, but not what we're looking for.

"Wait, what's that?" Marcos points at a small blurb in the lower right corner of page 9.

Yoona reads it out loud:

Community Reminder: The next school district meeting is on Tuesday, April 13, at 5:00 p.m. The agenda with predetermined topics can be accessed by calling the number below. New discussion topics are welcome, and one representative per subject will be invited to speak to the board. Please call 555-374-3872 for more information.

"There you go," the librarian says with a satisfied look on his face. "The next board meeting is nine days from now."

I do a quick calculation in my head—the meeting is three days before camp registration forms are due. If the board agrees to fund ESL classes for the next school year at that meeting, Vivian won't have to go to Evergreen Prep for more English help. She'd be getting it from Pacific Park Middle for free, which means her family will have enough money to pay for summer camp.

There's still a chance Camp Rock Out could happen for me and Vivian.

This is good. Really good.

We thank him for his help and head back to our table.

"Okay, we have nine days before the meeting," Yoona says. "That's not a lot of time."

I think out loud. "We need to gather as many signatures as we can this week. If we give them to Principal Klein by Friday, she'll have the weekend and Monday to get ready to talk to the board."

"Yeah, that makes sense," Yoona agrees.

"Great. How are we going to get signatures? Like, pin the petitions up around school or something like that?" I ask.

Marcos shrugs. "It'll be faster if we talk to kids directly, don't you think?"

I turn to him in surprise. "Walk up to them and ask? But I don't know most of the kids at school."

"I don't, either. But it's no big deal. I'm sure most of them would be up for it." He shrugs.

Wow. I'm definitely starting to see Marcos in a totally different way. There's something about how chill and relaxed he is that's worth admiring. He's like the opposite of me, always trying to live up to other people's expectations.

There's a lot I can learn from this skater boy.

For the adult signatures, I suggest hitting up parents in the after-school carline, and Marcos says we could also go to grocery stores or hang out in front of the local church.

The idea of walking up to strangers makes my stomach queasy. What if someone mentions what I'm doing to my family? But I try to channel Marcos's energy and tell myself it'll be all right.

I have to do this for Vivian.

I hold up my hand for a high five. "All right, we have a plan! Let's kick it off tomorrow, first thing in the morning."

Yoona slaps my hand, cheering. "Meet you two at the bike racks around seven thirty? I've done some early morning tutoring sessions before, and kids start to come in around then."

The three of us grin at each other. "Seven thirty it is."

Robot: initiate suffragette sequence. Beep boop bop.

CHAPTER
24

THE NEXT DAY, I HEAD to school early to meet Yoona and Marcos. I've never been at school this early, and it's kind of fun to see kids come in slowly and sloth-like.

Marcos approaches the first group of girls, all eighth graders walking onto campus together. They have big silver hoops in their ears and wear bright neon T-shirts with faded blue jeans and black-and-white checkered sneakers. After Marcos waves them down, they listen to his pitch.

"There are lots of kids coming to Pacific Park from other countries, and they need some help learning English. But Principal Klein says there's no money. Will you sign this petition so we can convince her to ask the school district for the funding?"

The tallest girl with short, curly hair tied up on one side snaps a bubble with pink gum and signs the petition. "Yeah, that makes sense."

"Well, duh, if someone needs help with their schoolwork, why wouldn't the school give them that?" Another girl with a bandana on her head takes the pen.

I want to hug each and every one of them.

A pair of sixth graders cruise by us and stop at the bike racks. One's got a trumpet case strapped to his back, and the other's got a violin.

I don't have Marcos's cool, skater-boy attitude, so my strategy is to use my status as Sixth Grade Student of the Year. It might help people see how serious we are and reassure them that they won't get in trouble for signing.

The last thing a Student of the Year would do is get in trouble.

I approach the two boys with my clipboard in hand. "Hi, do you have a minute?" I ask.

The two boys exchange glances. "Uh, sure. What's up?" the one with round glasses says.

I take a deep breath. "I'm Lily, and I was Sixth Grade Student of the Year. I'm petitioning Principal Klein to fund ESL classes for Pacific Park Middle students who have moved here from a different country and need a credentialed teacher to teach them English. Will you sign in support of this idea?"

"Sure!" The boy responds. "My mom is French, so I get what it's like to have different languages at home. And George's family is from Colombia."

Just like that, I've gotten my first signatures.

Not too shabby for a shy, awkward robot.

By the time the bell rings, we've gotten twenty-four signatures from Pacific Park Middle kids.

"Hey, we need adult signatures, too," I call out to Marcos and Yoona as we head toward our first period classes. "Don't forget to ask your teachers!"

When I show the petition to Mr. Silvers at the end of the day, he reads it carefully, then peers up at me. "I'm impressed you've taken the initiative here, Lily. I must say, it's not like you."

I hold back a sigh. There it is again, someone skeptical about me deciding to stand up and speak out.

"Actually, it *is* like me. It's just a side of me you've never seen before," I say. Because I do defend my family, like I tried to do that time at the supermarket with Ah-ma.

I just haven't brought this part of me to Pacific Park Middle.

"Well, you're quite an inspiration," he says as he signs the petition. "This makes me wonder if I should have done more to help these ESL kids, the way *you* are. I'm so glad to see you standing up for what you believe in, like Samuel Westing did in *The Westing Game*."

I don't tell him that for me, this is more about the Hoos, who were actually the first Asian American characters I ever read about in an English-language book. I'm fighting especially hard for Madame Hoo who, like Vivian, didn't speak a lot of English in the story and wasn't taken seriously because of it.

I just smile at Mr. Silvers and take the clipboard back.

Next up, the carline.

This robot is on a mission.

It turns out to be much harder to get parents to help.

"You've chosen to come to America, and the best way to become American is to assimilate. That means you immigrants should experience school like the other American kids, without special treatment," one mom in a fancy silver Mercedes says. "Plus, what's more American than speaking English?"

Neither Marcos nor I have a chance to tell her that we *are* American before she rolls her dark-tinted car window up. Or that there are plenty of places around the world that are *not* America whose people speak English. Like the UK, Canada, Australia, and New Zealand. Not to mention the Philippines, Singapore, Guam, even India.

Then Logan walks by, throws us a dirty look, and hops into the car.

Ugh. Guess the apple doesn't fall far from the tree.

Even some of the ESL Homework Club kids' parents don't join the cause. They say things like "It's not our place to challenge the school" or "We need to do our best with the opportunities we already have" or "Our kids just need to work a little harder."

These are things Dad, Mom, or Ah-ma would say.

Every "no" we get makes me worry that we're not doing the right thing. This could backfire and get us in real trouble.

I have no choice, though, but to keep going.

Because if we don't do it, no one else will.

CHAPTER
25

IT'S THURSDAY AFTERNOON, AND THE last car pulls away from the pickup line. Yoona waves me and Marcos over to the front steps, and I plop down next to her.

We've been gathering signatures since Monday. Every morning we approach kids from a different school entrance, and every afternoon we hit up the carlines. I told my family that I had a group project I had to work on after school every day this week, so they've been fine with me not rushing home to do my homework.

It doesn't feel good to lie. But this is important.

It's quiet as we count through the stacks of paper in our hands.

"I have 114 signatures and phone numbers," Yoona

declares, handing her petition copies to me.

"And 145 from me," Marcos says.

I count the last page on my clipboard. "As for me, I've got 123. That brings us to a total of . . . 382! With about seven hundred kids at Pacific Park Middle, and parents and teachers, too, that's a pretty good number."

We give each other a round of high fives, and the weight of a ginormous bag of rice lifts off my shoulders. There's no way Principal Klein can say no now.

"Should we bring them up to the front office today?" Yoona wonders out loud. "I think most teachers and administrators go home early on Fridays, so this afternoon might be our best chance before the board meeting next Tuesday."

Now? My heart beats faster at the thought.

Then my brain takes over. The only thing we're doing is showing Principal Klein that lots of people think that ESL classes are a good idea.

Plus, it has to be now. I need to get these ESL classes locked in quick before the Camp Rock Out registration or Evergreen tuition checks are due.

During all this, poor Vivian's been stuck at home, cut off from any social time that might "distract" her from her studies.

It's the pits. Thinking about Vivian makes me more determined than ever to make this work.

I gather our petition papers together into a big stack. "Yes, let's do it. But wait a sec." I pull out my trusty Discman from my backpack and wave it in the air. "Let's get into the vibe first."

Marcos laughs, and Yoona throws me a thumbs-up. "Great idea," Marcos says. "I've got a headphone splitter so we can listen with two sets of earphones."

The three of us settle into a corner, and I plug in our earphones. Marcos and Yoona share one set, and I skip ahead in the album to Pearl Jam's "Alive."

I close my eyes. My pounding heart needs a reminder of why I'm doing this. Like Keiko does when she gets up onstage.

I'm shining a light into the darkness. I'm making a change happen, not waiting for it.

My fingers move like they're practicing my ruler-guitar, and I try to remember what it felt like to have Keiko's guitar around my shoulders. As the last chords of Mike McCready's guitar solo fade away, I take a deep breath. "Okay, let's do this," I declare, blinking against the bright Pacific Park sun. Marcos and Yoona cheer, and together we walk to Principal Klein's office.

When Marcos pushes open the first door, Ms. Jensen's on the phone. She waves us in and motions us to knock.

"Here goes nothing," I say, pulling my shoulders back. "Ready?"

"Ready!" Marcos and Yoona say at the same time.

I knock on Principal Klein's office door.

"Come in."

I pull on the door handle, and we file in. Principal Klein is sitting behind her desk, flipping through papers. When she sees us, her eyebrows shoot up and her fingers pause in midair. "Why, hello, you three. What can I do for you?"

I clear my throat. "We have a request for you, Principal Klein." I hand her our stack of signatures.

"What's this?" Principal Klein takes them and reads the first page. "A petition for ESL support?"

"Yes, Principal Klein. The kids and adults who have signed it support giving students who need it a little extra help with their English."

Principal Klein skims through the pages with a look on her face that I can't read. Then she places them on her desk and leans forward in her chair.

Her blue eyes land on mine. "Tell me, what would you like me to do with this petition?"

I fumble for words. "We're hoping that you will reconsider asking the school board for money to pay for ESL classes at Pacific Park Middle."

Her gaze stays laser-focused on me. "I thought we came to an understanding the last time we talked about this, Lily. At Pacific Park Middle, we follow an

English-only approach to language learning."

I swallow down the ball of doubt that's risen into my throat.

Be like Eddie. Be like Pandora's Box.

"I understand, Principal Klein," I say. "But I still think there's more the school can do. Look at how many kids and adults at Pacific Park Middle agree. Can't we try something else?"

"I told you before. Budgets are tight. We can't provide kids with extra support. Finding and training teachers who can teach English to kids who don't speak it . . . it's a lot of work." Principal Klein's chair squeaks as she leans back.

"You can take it to the school district at the board meeting next week," I say. I can't hold back the note of defiance that makes it into my voice.

"I don't understand," Principal Klein says, shaking her head. She looks at me and Yoona pointedly. "The two of you are at the top of the class. You're both examples of how this is a society where those who work hard enough get what they deserve."

My face flushes. Yes, I've worked hard, and so has Yoona. But so have a lot of other kids, like Marcos, Carlos, Woojin, and Min. And of course, Vivian.

I realize that with her last comment, Principal Klein totally left Marcos out. I glance over at him, and he's got a scowl on his face. His blazing eyes meet mine. *Patience, Marcos,* I try to say to him through my gaze. He takes a deep breath, and his face softens into his usual chill look. But there's still a flash of anger in his eyes.

"Apparently hard work can only take you so far," I insist. "It's not fair that ESL kids are expected to do as well as the other kids do, when they are at a disadvantage. You're expecting them to learn a whole new language on top of what everyone else is studying. What they deserve is real help."

Yoona chimes in. "Principal Klein, the three of us have been trying to tutor a bunch of the students here at Pacific Park Middle. I found some workbooks at the library, and we've been going through them."

"We've tried lots of things to help our friends and family," I add. "Like putting together vocab lists."

"That's a nice demonstration of initiative, Yoona and Lily." Principal Klein nods approvingly.

She's ignored Marcos again. But this time, I don't need to look at him to know what he's feeling. Instead, my words tumble out to defend him. "Marcos is a big part of this, too," I say. "He's been demonstrating a lot of initiative, too, Principal Klein."

Her eyes shift to him quickly; then a mask falls over her face as she turns her attention back to me and Yoona.

Out of the corner of my eye, I see Marcos stand a little

straighter, a small smile on his face. Yoona continues. "The problem is, we don't know what to do next. We could use some help from someone who knows what they're doing. Like a real teacher."

"They deserve more than what we can give them, Principal Klein," I say as assertively as I can. "Please, will you help us?"

Principal Klein's eyes bounce between me, Yoona, and Marcos.

Finally, she pats our stack of petition papers and sighs. "I'll see what I can do."

"You mean you'll talk to the school board?" I ask hopefully.

Her gaze breaks away from mine. "I'll talk to some people, yes. I'll call you when I've got more to share."

I don't want to come across as smug and disrespectful in front of the principal, so I do my best to hold back the giant grin that's about to burst onto my face. But once we file out of her office and step outside, I can't keep it in.

"Whoop, whoop!" I cheer. "We did it!"

I can't believe it worked.

Marcos raises up his hand, and we exchange high fives. "I think this will make a real difference! Finally!"

"Totally," Yoona adds. She puts her hand to her chest. "It'll take a lot of pressure off us if this works!"

"Yeah, maybe she'll finally do what her students need." Marcos grins. "And thank you, Lily, for not letting her get away with ignoring me." He nudges my shoulder shyly.

I smile back. "She's got to know that skater boys have something to say, too."

"Oh, and I have something to share with you two, also!" Yoona pulls her sketchbook out of her backpack and flips it open.

My jaw drops. It's an amazing manga-style drawing of the three of us, each as a different superhero. Marcos soars through the air with a mask on his face and rockets on his skateboard, and I'm on top of a huge building and jamming on a guitar with fire bursts exploding behind me. Instead of superhero boots on my feet, she's drawn a pair of black boots like the ones I always wear, and instead of a bright red Superman cape, mine is red-and-black-checkered flannel.

Yoona has drawn herself like Wonder Woman, with long, wavy black hair and a snazzy crown, and she's aiming her drawing pencils out of the page like lasers.

"Wow," Marcos exclaims. "I had no idea you could draw like that."

"Looks like each one of us is full of hidden surprises." I grin. "We just need to take the time to discover them. Your drawing is sick, Yoona."

Yoona giggles and bops me on the shoulder. "Sick is right, Lily."

My heart swells. It's nice that I've got real friends to lean on.

We wave goodbye and head off in separate directions to our homes.

We've done what we can. It's up to Principal Klein now. I hope with my whole heart that her talk with the school board goes well.

CHAPTER
26

WHEN I GET HOME, DAD is sitting at the dining table with a cup of tea, and Ah-ma's got her hand on his, patting it slowly.

Something's going on.

"Hey, Dad. What are you doing home from work so early?" I drop my backpack to the floor and join them at the table.

His eyes seem to take a second to register my presence.

Weird.

"Hey, Lily," he finally says. "I came home early because I got some bad news at work today."

"Uh-oh. What happened?"

He shakes his head slowly. "I didn't get the promotion."

"Oh no," I breathe out. I scoot into the seat next to him. "Why not?"

Dad stares into his teacup. "My boss decided to promote someone who showed more . . . what's the word he used?" He squints his eyes in thought. "Oh, right." He curls two fingers on each hand and wiggles them like quotation marks. "Someone with more initiative."

Principal Klein used the same word with the three of us earlier this afternoon.

"What does that word mean, exactly?" Ah-ma wonders out loud.

Dad wraps his hands around his tea and takes a slow sip. "When you have initiative, it means that you see what's needed and you take charge without other people telling you to do it. I guess they thought I wasn't confident enough to take a new idea and make it happen."

Ouch. That's gotta hurt. I put my arms around his shoulders—navy polo shirt today—and give him a tight hug. "I'm sorry, Dad."

He takes off his glasses and rubs his eyes. "In Taipei, at school, they taught us that being loyal, respectful, and taking the time to build the right relationships was how to be a good employee. I thought making sure everyone was on board with my idea, even my boss, was what I needed to do before moving forward. You know, make everyone comfortable. But here . . ." He shakes his head. "It's different. My boss's boss thought I should have pushed my idea harder, even though some people weren't sure about it, because it was the right thing to do for the company."

I glance at Ah-ma. She was the one who told him to keep his head down and not share his idea without the approval of his boss. Does she regret it?

Ah-ma looks sad and confused, too. But she doesn't say anything. She pours Dad another cup of tea instead.

We sit together in silence until Ah-ma gets up to start preparing dinner.

I guess we're each trying to figure out how and when to speak up, even my father.

I sure hope my plan goes better than his did.

Dinner today is steamed cod, sauteed water spinach, dry tofu with edamame, and our usual white rice. The adults are quieter than usual, and today Ah-ma puts the biggest, juiciest pieces of cod in Dad's bowl, not mine.

I have no problem with that, though. Dad could use as many good vibes as he can get today.

After I help Mom wash the dishes and load them into the dishwasher to dry, the adults head into the living room to watch tapes of their soap opera. I go to my bedroom to do homework and listen to music.

I'm trying to figure out the relationship between a gene and DNA when a hand suddenly taps my shoulder. I jump, pulling my headphones off with a jerk. "Argh!"

It's Mom.

"Sorry, I kept knocking, but you didn't answer. You have a phone call," she says, pointing at the hallway. "It's a boy. . . . Marcos something?"

I blush immediately. A boy's never called me at home before.

Mom looks at me with raised eyebrows. "Talk in the hallway, please."

I follow her out of my room. Once Mom disappears back into the living room and the sounds of the Chinese soap opera start up again, I cup my hand over the receiver and speak into it as softly as I can.

"Marcos?"

"Lily. We have a problem."

Uh-oh. There's an urgency to Marcos's voice I've never heard before.

"What's going on?"

"It's Principal Klein. She's going down the list of names on our petition and calling people. She's trying to convince them to retract their signatures."

My heart drops into my stomach. "What?!"

"She called my parents a few minutes ago. Apparently, she called my aunt and uncle earlier, too. Now they're super scared."

"Oh no." I let out a breath. "But can she do that? That's not why we gathered signatures and phone numbers."

"She's the principal of Pacific Park Middle, Lily. She can do what she wants."

My head spins. Principal Klein lied to us. She lied to me. And now she's using our hard work and the people who have joined our cause against us.

Suddenly, I hear a click on the phone. It's the call-waiting.

It couldn't be . . . ?

"Hold on a sec, Marcos. . . ." I press and quickly let go of the flashing button to answer the second call.

"Hello, this is Lily Xiao speaking."

"Lily, this is Principal Klein. Could you please put your parents on the line?"

Oh no. It's her.

"Good evening, Principal Klein." I try to make my voice as calm and innocent as possible. But my heart is pounding at super speed. "May I ask what this is about?"

Could Marcos be wrong? Maybe Principal Klein isn't calling because she's angry about the petition. Maybe she's calling for a whole different reason.

"You know what this is about, Lily. Please get them now."

Alert, alert! Danger! Danger!

For a split second, my impulse is to hang up the phone.

But I don't dare.

"One second, Principal Klein."

Before getting my parents, though, I click back into my conversation with Marcos.

"Principal Klein's on the other line right now, Marcos," I tell him. "She wants to talk to my parents."

"Oh no," he breathes into the phone. "I think we're in trouble, Lily."

I swallow down the lump in my throat. "I think you're right, Marcos."

I click back to the line that Principal Klein is on, place the receiver on the hallway table, and reluctantly head into the living room.

Mom and Dad are sitting together on the couch, and Ah-ma's rocking back and forth in the wicker armchair with a blanket on her lap. Their eyes are fixed on the TV against the living room wall, where there's a scene of an emperor and empress presiding at the front of the ancient Chinese imperial court. A woman dressed in a beautiful qí páo kneels in front of them, probably praying for leniency for something she's done that the emperor and empresses don't approve of.

I know the feeling.

I take a deep breath. "Mom, Dad. Principal Klein's on the phone in the hallway. She wants to speak to one of you."

All three of their heads spin faster than in that *Exorcist* movie that Mom and Dad were watching one night when I was supposed to be in bed.

"The principal is calling? What's this about?" Dad clicks the remote to pause the video and stands up, a worried look on his face.

I don't want to stay for the truth bomb that's about to come.

Without a word, I turn so I can escape to my room. But I catch a glimpse of Ah-ma's face.

It's ashen, like she's seen a ghost.

Ah-ma's going to be so disappointed in her disobedient granddaughter who has incurred the anger of the top authority of her school.

All because of my wild dream to be a grunge rocker.

And my attempt to speak up for myself and what I want, for once.

Robot: stand by for possible shutdown sequence.

CHAPTER
27

DAD FOLLOWS ME TO THE hallway and picks up the phone, eyes staring at me as he speaks into it.

"Hello, Principal Klein. It's Steven Xiao, Lily's father. How can I help you?"

I shut the door to my bedroom. I don't want to hear Dad's reaction as Principal Klein tells him about what I've done.

But is it really that wrong? All I did was start a petition.

Although I did it after my family told me not to do anything about this ESL thing.

Behind the door, I hear muffled sounds as Dad speaks to Principal Klein. Then it's silent for a few seconds.

The door creaks open, and Dad pokes his head in.

"Lily, please come out here. We need to talk." His voice is stern and still.

"Yes, Dad," I nervously reply, and shuffle behind him to the living room.

"What's going on, lǎo gōng?" Mom asks, looking worried. Ah-ma's practically a ghost by how pale her face has become.

Dad gestures at me to take the armchair, then sits next to Mom on the loveseat. "Lily, tell us what you've been up to. Please start at the very beginning, from that night after you and Vivian got your progress grades in the mail."

I stare at the seams of the pillow in my arms. "Last week, I went to Principal Klein to ask her if she'd give Vivian some extra tutoring for English."

"You talked to your principal? After your father said not to?" Ah-ma says breathlessly.

"Wait, Ma. There's more." Dad looks at me angrily.

I take a deep breath. "After she said no, I started a petition with some kids at school to ask her to reconsider. We want her to go to the school board to ask for the funding the school needs to provide ESL classes."

"A petition? What is that?" Ah-ma asks.

"It's when you ask people to sign a paper that has a statement of change on it," Dad responds, eyes still fixated on me. "You use those signatures as leverage when you approach the authority who can change the rules."

Ah-ma looks confused. "I don't understand. What's the point of doing that?"

"It's to challenge an existing policy or law," Dad explains.

Ah-ma stares at me with horror on her face. "Oh, Lily. You didn't."

"But organizing petitions is something that people do here. It's not that big of a deal," I say.

"I'd say it was a big deal, Lily. Over three hundred signatures? That's a lot of people in Pacific Park," Dad says. "How did you even think of this idea?"

Mom's eyebrows rise up. "Three hundred? Wow," she whispers. Ah-ma shoots her a look, and Mom's eyes quickly shift away.

"I learned about it in social studies, as a part of the women's suffrage movement project. We asked kids at school and parents in the carline to sign."

"The carline? After school?" Dad asks, a puzzled expression on his face.

Oops.

"Lily, you lied to us about your after-school project," he says sternly.

"This *was* my after-school project." I avoid his eyes and pick at the threads of the pillow.

There's more than guilt in my stomach, though. I feel a bit of . . . pride.

I know I shouldn't have done all this behind my family's back. That was wrong. But what I've done is a pretty big deal, even if Principal Klein has completely sabotaged the whole thing.

Over three hundred signatures is something.

I'm sure Pandora's Box would agree. So would Eddie Vedder.

I jut my chin. "Dad, putting together petitions is a part of American history. It's a way to show authorities that a lot of people care about something and want change. It's not supposed to get you in trouble or anything if you start it or sign it."

"Starting petitions is something that Taiwanese people don't do, though," Ah-ma says with a sharp tone. "We mustn't cause any trouble. We're lucky to be here, and we should be grateful. The least we can do is keep our heads down and accept what we have. Son, is Lily in trouble now for doing this?"

"No, she's not being punished," Dad assures her. "But, Lily," he says, turning back toward me, "I asked you not to do anything. I told you I'd handle it."

A flash of anger burns through me. "By sending Vivian to Evergreen?"

Dad's eyes open wide with surprise. "How did you know about that?"

"Vivian overheard her parents talking about it."

Dad shrugs. "Changing schools is a perfectly reasonable solution. Don't you want Vivian to get the help she needs?"

"I do, but I don't want her to switch schools." My mind whirls for something, anything, that could keep Vivian at Pacific Park. "Wait, I know. What if Auntie and Uncle use the Camp Rock Out money for English tutoring instead? Then Vivian and I can keep going to Pacific Park Middle together."

Not going to Camp Rock Out would be awful. But not as awful as not going to school with my best friend anymore.

Dad shakes his head. "The money they'll save from not sending Vivian to camp isn't enough to pay for a whole year of private tutoring. We did the math. . . . It's more economical to send Vivian to Evergreen than pay for the same amount of private tutoring she'll need if she stayed at Pacific Park. There's a good chance that Vivian will get the financial aid I helped Auntie and Uncle apply for."

"So that's it?" I plead. "What if the school board decides to fund ESL classes at Pacific Park Middle? Could she stay?"

"That'd change the calculations for sure. But that's not going to happen. Principal Klein made it clear in her phone call that her policy at Pacific Park Middle is to support an English-only approach to language learning."

An impossible idea flashes into my head.

"What if *I* went to talk to the school board?"

Dad's mouth drops open, and Mom's eyes widen to the size of two rice bowls.

Ah-ma sits straight up in her chair. "Absolutely not, Lily. I forbid it."

"Why not, Ah-ma? It's not fair that Principal Klein is the one deciding whether or not the board hears our case. It's not fair that the only way Vivian gets what she needs is to change schools and make our family pay a ton of money," I say firmly. "And what about other kids with families where private school isn't an option? We should fight for what everyone deserves, even if it means getting up in front of the school board and making a case for what's right."

"Lily, that is not how we do things in the Xiao family," Dad insists, his back straighter than usual.

"But I don't want to do things the way the Xiao family does. I want to do things my way!" I insist.

"Lily!"

The sharpness of Ah-ma's tone makes me jump. She glares at me, hands clasped in front of her. "Stop this. This is not how you speak to your family."

There it is again, what I should or shouldn't do. I'm so tired of it.

"Why not? What could possibly go wrong if we asked?" I shout.

"You could disappear forever, like your grandfather did!"

Ah-ma's words make me recoil in my chair, like a huge wave has washed over me and pinned me against its back.

My grandfather? What is Ah-ma talking about?

Mom gasps, her hands covering her mouth, and Dad stares at Ah-ma with big, worried eyes. Mine ping-pong between my parents before landing back on Ah-ma, who's still staring at me with anger all over her face.

Or is it fear?

I dare myself to ask. "What do you mean, Ah-ma?"

"I will tell you why you must keep your head down. I will tell you why you mustn't get up in front of that school board."

"Ma, please, don't. Don't put yourself through it again," Dad pleads.

She glares at him. "I must. If it will make Lily understand, I will tell her." Ah-ma looks into my eyes. "I can't protect her anymore."

Tingles start to travel up and down my spine. I have no idea what's about to come.

Ah-ma's gaze turns distant, and she clasps her hands in front of her tightly. "My husband was working for the Taiwanese army as a translator when your dad was born. Life in Taiwan at that time was very difficult.

When Japan was forced to give Taiwan up after World War II, the Kuomintang government from China fled to the island. They had lost the civil war to the Chinese Communists and came to Taiwan to regroup.

"At first, we welcomed the KMT and the change they promised to bring. But they were so focused on winning back China and battling the Communists that the government saved everything they could for the war effort. As things got worse and worse for the Taiwanese, with food shortages and no jobs, people started to speak up. People like Ah-gong, your grandfather. My husband."

Ah-ma's face softens, and tears fill her dark and brooding eyes. "Your dad wasn't even a year old when the KMT soldiers came to take Ah-gong away. I begged for his release at the police station, but they wouldn't listen. Later, they told us that he'd attended a rally to fight for more rights for the Taiwanese. Because he was speaking out against the government, they said it meant he was a Communist, that he was an enemy."

I suck in my breath. "Ah-ma. I had no idea."

"He never came back." Ah-ma's gaze is as sharp as an eagle's. "Can you see now why you cannot do these things, Lily? Can you see what can happen if you speak up?"

I swallow down the lump in my throat. My head whirls with a mix of sadness and shame for what happened, and for making Ah-ma relive it all over again.

I glance at my dad, who never got to know his own father.

"Now you know, Lily, why we are so careful," Dad says softly. He pulls at the collar of his polo shirt and rubs the back of his neck. "Not only was my father taken away forty years ago, but when I was growing up, the government censored newspaper articles, denied us the right to assemble, even forbade us to speak in Taiwanese. The only music we got to listen to was patriotic music. We didn't have the freedom to listen to whatever we wanted, like you get to do."

I can't imagine being forced to listen to "The Star-Spangled Banner" all day. I mean, it's a powerful song, but still.

It's no Pearl Jam.

"Even now, people are still being arrested for pushing for democracy in Taiwan," Dad continues. "Martial law was lifted in Taiwan only five years ago. Freedom of speech isn't a right there . . . yet. We have to be careful about what we say."

The pieces of the puzzle fall into place. This is why my family is always so afraid to speak up. From Dad not wanting to get his boss annoyed to my parents insisting on keeping my bedroom walls clean for the landlord to Ah-ma not fighting against that horrible man at the grocery store . . . they're avoiding any kind of conflict.

Because to them, conflict has big consequences.

I'm afraid to meet Ah-ma's gaze, so I stare at my hands. "I had no idea this had happened."

"That's one of the reasons we left," Mom chimes in. "We wanted to have a child in a place where you have opportunities and freedoms that your dad and I didn't."

I suddenly feel both grateful and lucky that we are Americans.

But something still doesn't make any sense.

"I'm glad that we live here now, where we have more freedom," I say. "But like you said, things are different here. We're supposed to speak up when we think something isn't right."

"No, Lily," Ah-ma interrupts. "Let it go. If you care for us, you will stop this fight of yours."

"But, Ah-ma, you want me to help Vivian, right? This is the way I've chosen to help. She really needs it," I protest. "We have to do something!"

Ah-ma gets up from her chair and stands tall in front of me. "Your ah-gong spoke up, and he's gone. I will not have the same thing happen to my granddaughter. I don't care where we are right now or why you're doing it. It's not worth it."

"Ma . . ." Dad starts to say.

"That's enough. The conversation is over." Her hands come down to her sides and curl into fists, like she's a soldier. Then she turns and heads into her bedroom, her flowery blouse whipping behind her dramatically.

Dad looks as surprised as I am. But he recovers quickly and turns his attention back to me.

"Lily, I don't want to argue about this anymore. At the end of the day, you did what we told you not to do, and in a very public, dangerous way. You lied to us. This is not what we taught you. This is not how we expect you to behave. And now that you know where we're coming from, you should understand why."

There are those words again. "Expect." "Should."

It's always about what *they* expect, what they think *I* should do.

When am I finally going to get to do what I want, what I think is right? Did they tell me this horrible story about Ah-gong, about life in Taipei under martial law, to get me to stop going down the path I've chosen and take theirs instead?

A rage starts to burn in my chest, and my heart pounds. It gets stronger and stronger, like the opening riffs of a grunge rock song. But not of a deep, soulful ballad.

It's the heavy, distorted chords of a loud, angry, scream-into-the-mic grunge song.

What's in my heart explodes through my voice.

"No, Dad. No, Mom!" I yell. "I'm so sick of always

doing what you want me to do. I do what you expect all the time." I jab at the air with my pointer finger. "I get the grades, I get the awards. But I don't do the fun stuff that normal kids get to do after school because I'm expected to come home to study. And I don't complain, I just do it." Tears spring to my eyes, and I wipe them clumsily with the back of my hand.

"When is it enough?" I sniff, my anger melting into shame. "When am I going to be allowed to be me? All you want from me is perfect grades, for me to do what you want. But can't you see that I want to be more than that?"

Mom and Dad stare at me, too stunned to speak.

Not that I expect them to say anything, anyway.

I spin around and storm into my room, slamming the door behind me. I frantically look for my Pearl Jam CD, and when I finally find it, I jam it in my stereo and turn the volume up high.

I hit Play. The frenzied, nervous energy of the opening guitar riff of "Once" starts, and Eddie's angry lyrics hit my ears right away. His deep wailing lingers before it builds into a loud, harsh screech. The music pounding the walls of my bedroom perfectly captures the rage I'm feeling.

I finally did it. I channeled Eddie and his intense, growling energy and spoke up. I yelled, I shouted, I said things that came from the heart and with a ton of real feeling. My robot self is officially gone, replaced by an emotional being who says—no, screams—what she feels inside.

It's what I've been wanting to do all this time, ever since I discovered Camp Rock Out.

So why does it feel so horrible?

CHAPTER
28

I HIT THE SNOOZE BUTTON a third time, then curl back into the sheets and squeeze my eyes shut to block out the light shining through the window shades.

I'm super late for school already. And I bet my parents are worried sick about that inevitable tardy.

But I don't care. Even though I finally said what was on my mind last night, I still failed my family, I failed Ah-ma, and I failed Vivian.

And Marcos, Yoona, and the kids and parents who signed our petition.

I've turned from Lily Xiao, invisible class robot, into Lily Xiao, in-your-face class mess-up.

And it's all my fault. The petition was my idea. I lied to my family, and when I suggested that I go talk to the school board myself, I made Ah-ma relive a horrible memory about her husband.

I can't go there again. Not if it hurts Ah-ma the way I did last night.

Someone knocks softly on my bedroom door. "Lily? Are you okay?"

I burrow deeper into my covers and don't say a word.

Mom sighs from behind the door. "Dad and I need to go to work. Breakfast is on the table. We'll talk tonight."

Her steps move away from my bedroom, and I squeeze my eyes shut again. By the time the alarm rings for the fourth time, I know I can't avoid life anymore. I have a feeling my parents will be able to stomach a tardy, but not an unexcused absence.

I drag myself out of bed, throw on some clothes, and trudge into the hallway. Then I glance in the direction of Ah-ma's room.

The door is shut.

I find a bowl of rice porridge on the dining table. But it's turned into the consistency of glue.

Nope. Not today.

Then I face the fridge and take a deep breath.

Did Ah-ma make me and Vivian biàn dangs for school lunch today, like she does every morning? Or have I made her so angry that she can't do it?

Or worse, won't?

I pull the fridge door open . . .

And two silver boxes sit neatly on the fridge shelf.

My heart feels lighter and heavier at the same time.

Ah-ma always comes through, even the day after her granddaughter made her relive the worst memory of her life.

I stuff them into my backpack and get onto my bike to head to school.

When I cruise up to Pacific Park Middle, I head straight to the main office for a tardy slip. Luckily, while I wait for Ms. Jensen to write one up for me, the door to Principal Klein's office is open and I can see that she's not there.

I want to avoid her for as long as I possibly can. I can't believe she betrayed us like that.

I take the tardy slip to first-period social studies. Ms. King glances at it quickly when I hand it to her and continues lecturing about World War II. When I take my seat next to Yoona, she squeezes my arm. "Are you okay?" she whispers.

I shake my head and bury it in my arms for the rest of class. Yoona's sympathy only makes me feel worse. It doesn't seem like she's mad at me.

But she should be.

The bell finally rings, and I grab my backpack and book it out of there as fast as I can.

"Wait, Lily!" Yoona calls out from behind me. But I don't turn back. I can't face her.

I keep my head down the best I can all morning.

There's no way to avoid Vivian at lunchtime, though, or else she'll literally go hungry. When I walk into our courtyard with Ah-ma's biàn dangs, Vivian's waiting for me. She leaps up from the bench and bounces over, wrapping me in a huge hug.

"I heard about what happened last night, biǎo jiě!" she exclaims. "I can't believe Principal Klein did that."

"I'm so sorry I couldn't make the ESL classes happen for you, biǎo mèi," I say, tears filling my eyes. "Camp Rock Out, either."

"Oh, biǎo jiě." Vivan pulls me over to our bench and sits me down. "You tried and that's what's important."

"I thought she'd do the right thing. I thought the petition would change her mind, that things would be different. It's been for nothing." I wipe my wet cheeks with the back of my hand.

Vivian's silent for a moment. Then she speaks. "Biǎo jiě, you *have* changed things. You don't see it?"

I'm confused. "What do you mean?"

"You did something I never would have dreamed of doing. I never would have dared to stand up to the school like you and Marcos and Yoona did."

"Really? But you've always been way braver than I am."

"Maybe in Taipei when we were little. But it's different in Pacific Park. It's been so hard for me here." Vivian tucks her hair behind her ears. "I've been blaming

myself this whole time for not doing well in school."
She runs her finger down a crack in the concrete bench.
"With everything you're doing with this ESL thing,
you've helped me realize that me not doing well isn't
because I'm not working hard enough. The system has
to change, too."

"I had no idea you were blaming yourself so much."
I grab Vivian's hand and hold it tightly.

"It didn't help that Ah-ma and my parents kept pushing me. But I get it now, about how it's different here
in the US. When something's not right and you're not
getting what you think you deserve, we're allowed to
speak up. Even though I miss Taipei a ton and adjusting
to life here is still hard, living here in America is starting
to feel more and more like . . . home. A place that I'm
proud to be a part of, even though things aren't perfect.
And one of the best parts is that we can actually make
it better."

When my eyes meet Vivian's, I notice a peace in them
I haven't seen in a long time.

I don't know if I deserve the nice things Vivian is saying. But it makes the tightness in my chest loosen up the
tiniest bit.

"Thanks, biǎo mèi," I whisper gratefully. "I'm glad
you're feeling better about being in Pacific Park. I'm glad
you're here."

A pair of girls in matching plaid skirts wander by the

opening to the courtyard. When one of them spots me, she pulls on the sleeve of the other one and starts whispering as they walk away.

Well, I'm definitely not invisible anymore.

"Do you think all the kids at Pacific Park Middle hate me, biǎo mèi?" I ask, my eyes watching the girls disappear around the corner. "I got everyone in so much trouble."

Vivian shakes her head. "Absolutely not. In fact, a few kids have come up to me to ask how you're doing."

"You?" I'm surprised. Most kids seem to have figured out that Vivian doesn't speak much English. They rarely approach her unless I'm there.

"Yeah, it was kind of nice." She grins. "Maybe I should speak up more now, too."

"Not that speaking up gets you what you want," I mumble back.

Vivian links her arm with mine. "It's a huge bummer that the petition didn't work. And I know Ah-ma's sad, and that your parents don't get why you did what you did." She puts her head on my shoulder. "I know why you did it, though. For that, thanks. I hope you can be proud of what you tried to do."

Then Vivian rubs her belly and groans loudly, eyes sparkling. "And most importantly, you bring me lunch every day! I'm starving—let's dig in, biǎo jiě!"

I grin and pull out our biàn dangs and hand her one.

"Yeah," I say softly, as the scent of Ah-ma's food fills the courtyard. "I'll do my best to be proud of what I did."

It's true that I didn't get what I wanted from all this. There's no ESL at Pacific Park Middle, no Camp Rock Out, Vivian's changing schools, and Ah-ma is holed up in her room.

But something good has come out of it. My biǎo mèi is adjusting to life in Pacific Park.

Because of what I did.

The things you do for your family.

CHAPTER
29

AFTER LUNCH, WHEN I GLANCE around the crowded hallways on my way to fifth-period algebra, I notice a few sympathetic looks from kids. Even Ketchup Head bops me on the shoulder as he skates by me in front of the school gym.

"Hey, welcome to the bad kids club! We could use more girls like you," he calls out.

I roll my eyes at him. But I can't help smiling to myself. I know better now—he's not a member of the bad kids club, either, even though he's a skater boy.

Still, next time I have a chance to talk to him, I'm going to set him straight about his misguided assumption that Asians can't be into grunge and that we're only allowed to like violins or pianos.

At the bike racks after school, Vivian suggests that we stop by Power Records before heading home. "You look so sad, biǎo jiě. Maybe it'll cheer you up," she says.

"Okay, fine," I say, giving in. "I'm pretty sure Ah-ma wouldn't want to see me if I went home now, anyway."

Vivian starts to pedal toward Power Records, and I follow behind. When we get to the grunge section, Keiko's there, shelving CDs.

"Lily, Vivian!" she exclaims when she sees us, putting down the stack of CDs in her hands. "What's the update? Did you two sign up for your rock-and-roll camp yet?"

Vivian glances at me nervously. "Um, we not going to camp."

"What?!" Keiko splutters. "What happened?"

Vivian and I exchange looks, and Vivian gestures at me to continue. I take a deep breath and tell Keiko everything, from the deal I struck with our parents to forming the ESL Homework Club to Vivian's bad progress grade to Principal Klein sabotaging my petition to finally getting why our families are so hesitant to stand up to the school.

". . . Now there's no way Pacific Park Middle will get funding for ESL classes, and Vivian will have to go to Evergreen and move farther away."

"Wow, a ton has happened. It's awful that your principal won't go to the school board. And I'm sorry that

Vivian's parents aren't letting her go to the camp. But Lily, you could still go, couldn't you?" Keiko asks, a confused look on her face.

"I guess so," I say, glancing at Vivian. She avoids my eyes and stares at a record display instead. "But this is bigger than Camp Rock Out now. It's about what's right. It's about what the English learners at Pacific Park Middle deserve."

"Yeah, zhè yī diǎn dōu bù gong píng," Vivian mutters, complaining about how unfair this all is.

Hearing Vivian speak in Chinese in front of Keiko suddenly sparks a memory. "Wait, Keiko, you didn't speak English when you were a kid either, right?" I ask.

"No, I didn't. I was born in Osaka, Japan, and my dad moved us to San Francisco ten years ago after he got a job at an American company."

"So how did you learn English?"

"I went to a Japanese bilingual school," Keiko responds.

"A bilingual school? How did that work exactly?" I wonder out loud.

"Because bilingual education means that you're taught in both languages, my teachers were Japanese speakers. At the beginning, most of my classes were taught in Japanese, with maybe only an hour of English. Slowly, as I got better, we'd start to do more and more learning in English, until our English caught up to our Japanese."

"That sounds awesome!" I exclaim. "The best of both worlds. So how did the school come about?"

"It was founded by Japanese American parents who wanted their kids to hold on to their Japanese heritage, especially after World War II."

"A bunch of parents started it by themselves?" I ask in wonder. "How'd they pull that off?"

"Have you studied World War II yet in school?" Keiko asks.

I nod. "Yes, we're just starting that unit."

"You must know about the tens of thousands of Japanese Americans who were forced to leave their homes and live in the desert because we happened to be fighting Japan at the time, right?"

"Yeah," I say softly. "It was terrible of our government to do that to its own citizens."

"It was," Keiko says. "When they finally got to leave the camps and go home, a bunch of Japanese American parents from San Francisco were so angry about how they were treated that they demanded that the US government make it up to them somehow."

"They did?" I love the idea of more Asian Americans like me and Keiko standing up and asking for what we deserve.

"Yes, and one of their demands was for the government to do more to preserve and protect the Japanese culture here in the States." Keiko clenches her teeth and shakes her head angrily. "Those parents were *so* grunge. In fact, Joan and I are working on a new song about that period of history. Anyway, the parents got the funding they needed, and the rest is history."

"Principal Klein doesn't like the idea of bilingual education," I tell Keiko. "She thinks full English immersion is the best way for kids to learn, and that Vivian and I should be talking to each other, and our families, in English. But I don't want us to lose our Chinese. We'd have nothing to talk about!"

Keiko crinkles her nose. "Yeah, that's no good. The bilingual approach was a pretty great way to learn English while staying connected to Japanese and Japanese American culture. And other Japanese people."

"That sounds amazing. Even though Principal Klein insists on English only, it's just not working."

"Maybe you should keep fighting, then. Remember, grunge isn't only about music. It's also about doing and saying what needs to be said, even if it's ugly and raw and dark."

I stare down at my chunky leather boots. "Yeah, I get that. What if fighting for what's right hurts your family, though? My grandma's upset and scared about the whole standing up and speaking out thing. Apparently, you can't do that in Taiwan."

What happened to Ah-gong sticks into my brain like a needle. "When someone she loved tried to do that in the past, really bad things happened," I add softly.

"I get it," Keiko replies. She picks up a stack of CDs and starts to slot them on a shelf. "Internment was awful for Japanese Americans, too. But it was because it was so unfair that a lot of people took the risk and fought as hard as they did to preserve their cultures and identities, like starting the school or suing the government to get their land back."

She pauses for a minute and stares into the distance. "It's these types of stories that make me want to keep creating the kind of music I do. I don't want to be quiet and let things like that happen again. I want to be loud and bold and for people to pay attention to the things I have to say, so we can make things better and not repeat the bad parts of history."

Vivian hands Keiko another stack of CDs, and Keiko takes them from her, smiling gently. "I know how important family is and that we want them to feel safe and comfortable. But sometimes, you have to do what you think is right, for yourself, for your own sense of self-respect. You honor your family by being honest and clear about what you plan on doing."

I bite my lip. I know what is right. But should I keep fighting?

"Lily! I knew you'd be here!" A boy's voice calls out.

I spin around, and it's Marcos, his long eyelashes framing his worried eyes. Yoona's right behind him, her eyes big behind her blue glasses and her wavy hair flaring out in a way that makes her look frantic.

"I think your friends want to talk to you." Keiko smiles at me, squeezes my shoulder, and heads back to the information counter.

"Geez, Lily, avoid us much?" Yoona gasps as she bounces over to me and Vivian. "We've been trying to track you down all day. Are you okay? What did Principal Klein say to you? And your parents?"

I avoid their eyes, ashamed of everything that happened.

Vivian speaks up for me, as usual. "Lily is very sad. Our parents are not happy. But I feel proud. You do a good thing for me and for other kids. Even if it not work, it matters."

"Totally, Vivian," Yoona agrees. "We did a good thing. My parents didn't get mad after Principal Klein called them. In fact, we had a long talk about how lost I feel as a tutor. They're going to try and get me workbooks from Korea that are designed to help Korean kids learn English."

Marcos twirls a wheel on his skateboard. "Yeah, we tried, right? My aunt and uncle can't afford extra tutoring, though, and they don't speak English well enough themselves to do anything. My cousin will have to keep doing what he can, with my help." He shrugs, blowing his floppy hair away from his eyes.

Keiko's words are still ringing in my ears. This whole thing feels unfinished. None of the things that Marcos and Yoona are going to do sound fair to them. Teaching our loved ones English shouldn't be solely our responsibility. We're not real teachers. It's the school that should be stepping up to help.

It's time to shine light into the darkness. And do what I think is best.

I close my eyes and imagine myself onstage. I see bright spotlights and a band behind me.

But it's not an electric guitar in my hands.

It's a mic.

And in front of me isn't an audience of screaming fans. It's the school board, listening to me explain why the right thing to do is to provide ESL support for all English learners at Pacific Park Middle School.

I need to stop expecting other people to stand up for me, and then getting disappointed when they don't. I need to do more to change the things that I think need changing myself.

I also need to stop being what others expect me to be, whether it's an obedient daughter who doesn't cause trouble or a docile, grateful Student of the Year who doesn't use her privilege to speak up.

I need to become Lily Xiao, independent thinker, free to do what I expect of myself.

And what I expect of myself is to be what grunge stands for, inside and out.

I stand up as tall as my body can stretch.

"This isn't over. We need to go to the school district ourselves. We need to go to that board meeting," I announce.

The three of them stare at me, mouths hanging open.

"Nǐ xiǎng zuò shén me?" Vivian splutters.

"You seriously want us to go around Principal Klein and talk to the board on our own?" Marcos says, his eyes widening.

"Yes," I say firmly. "The board meeting is in four days. I'll speak for us. I know what I want to say."

Yoona plays nervously with one of her black curls. "Why? What if Principal Klein finds out and sabotages us again?"

"I need to finish what I've already started. I need to stop relying on other people to make change happen. I believe in this," I say. "I want to keep standing up for it. I'm the Student of the Year, remember? They'll listen to me."

"Man, that's so sick, Lily!" Marcos exclaims. "Gotta say, you're not who I thought you were. But I'm glad I was wrong."

"Woo-hoo!" Vivian cheers. "You can do it, biǎo jiě!"

I grin at her, my insides bubbling with pride. My biǎo mèi always has my back.

Yoona bounces up and down on her toes. "This is not only your fight, Lily. It's ours, too. Even if you're the one in front of the mic, we'll be there behind you."

My heart soars. We *are* like a real rock band.

Suddenly, Keiko interrupts us. "Hey, you kids like milkshakes?"

"Um, yeah?" Marcos responds, looking a bit confused.

"Why don't you go upstairs to the café and tell whoever is working the counter to make you each a milkshake, courtesy of Keiko Tanaka? You can talk more about how you're going to change the system up there." She winks at me and strikes a power pose. "Do it, Lily."

Keiko is so amazingly grunge.

Although maybe I'm not that far off, either.

"Thanks, Keiko." I wave at her gratefully and turn to head upstairs. But I stop for a second and pull on Marcos's sleeve. "By the way, Marcos, Keiko's the lead guitarist for Pandora's Box."

Marcos tilts his chin up, acknowledging her. "That's sweet. I play bass, actually."

Keiko grabs a flyer from the information desk and hands it to him. "We're playing next Saturday. You and your friends come watch, okay?"

I hope he brings Ketchup Head, too. Because seeing an all-girl band like Pandora's Box is going to help make sure he knows that girls like me and Vivian can be rockers, too.

Yoona, Vivian, Marcos, and I head upstairs to the Power Records café, and I order us chocolate-banana milkshakes from the lanky boy with yellow curls and an olive-green beanie at the counter. I pull out a notebook, and the four of us work on my speech together.

I don't try to copy Pearl Jam's or Pandora's Box's lyrics, though.

Instead, I channel my own beat. My own sound.

Finally, after a few drafts, I get to a speech that captures the things I want to say. Marcos, Yoona, Vivian, and I read it silently to ourselves one last time.

Yoona grins with satisfaction. "This is good, Lily. Really good."

Marcos agrees. "It's solid stuff."

"Nǐ zhǔn bèi hǎole." Vivian flashes me a double thumbs-up.

She's right. I'm ready.

I look at my band members and grin proudly. We can do this.

I can do this.

But there's one more conversation I need to have.

CHAPTER
30

WHEN I GET HOME, MOM and Dad are sitting quietly in the living room, a tray of tea in front of them on the coffee table. They turn their heads as I pull off my boots and shuffle my feet into slippers.

"Lily," Mom says, her eyes tired and concerned. "You're here."

I glance down the hallway to check on Ah-ma's door. Still shut.

I settle into the rocking chair and take a deep breath. "I need to talk to you two."

"Us too," Dad says, nervously pulling at the collar of his baby-blue polo.

The Xiao family clearly isn't used to these types of conversations. But maybe we need to change that.

I take a deep breath. "I'm sorry I lied to you about

what I was doing after school all week. I should have told you about the petition."

"Yes, you should have." Dad nods. "We also should have told you about our plans for Vivian. We shouldn't have hidden that from you."

Mom rubs her eyes, pours some tea into a cup, and hands it to me. "We were afraid how devastated you'd be, having Vivian move schools. We tried to protect you by waiting until it was final. I see now that we shouldn't have done that."

I stare down at my hands. "Yeah. It felt like some big secret I wasn't a part of."

"Sometimes we forget that you're a seventh grader now," Dad says. He looks at Mom. "I think we both need to work on trusting you a bit more. That means no more lies from you, either, though."

"I know. I'm sorry I did that. I just . . ." I want to explain why I did it, even though I knew I shouldn't have. But desperate times call for desperate measures . . . sometimes? "Is Vivian for sure going to Evergreen next year?" I ask.

Dad shakes his head. "Not yet. We're still waiting on that scholarship. Auntie and Uncle feel like Vivian needs help from real teachers, and that's not going to happen at Pacific Park Middle. If Evergreen is the only place to get that, that's where Vivian will go."

My stomach lurches at how final Dad's words sound. But it's not over yet.

"If the Pacific Park school board decides to fund ESL classes at Pacific Park Middle for the next school year, can Vivian stay?" I ask carefully.

"Well, that'd be ideal. But Principal Klein made it pretty clear to me last night that she won't be asking the school board to explore alternatives to full English immersion." Dad shrugs. "I don't think she'll change her mind."

"I don't think she will, either. And I don't want to lie to you anymore. So I have something to tell you." Mom and Dad look back at me, their eyes concerned and nervous.

A few days ago, when Marcos, Yoona, and I went to Principal Klein together and asked her to bring this subject up at the next board meeting, I listened to my inner voice for the first time, instead of listening to Ah-ma's. I stood up for myself in front of someone super intimidating, and I did it for Vivian, and for all the other ESL kids I've gotten to know.

I'm about to tell my parents that I'm going to do something scary, something I know they won't want me to do. I could save them from the worry I know they're going to feel and just keep it to myself.

But I want them to know who their daughter is . . . and what I'm capable of doing.

I take a deep breath. *From the chest, through the heart, and out through your voice.* "I'm going to go to the school district to ask for ESL funding myself."

Mom and Dad stare at me in shock.

"What?! You?" Mom manages to get out.

"Yes, me. There's a board meeting on Tuesday afternoon, and I want to ask for funding for ESL classes at Pacific Park Middle. I know it'll make you very nervous and that Ah-ma will be scared for me. But I'm going to do it."

"For Vivian? Oh, Lily, Vivian knows you've done everything you can. Our family history is her history, too," Dad says. "We already have a plan to help her."

I shake my head. "No, Dad, there's more that I can do, and this is it. Plus, this isn't only about getting Vivian what she needs. I need to do it for myself, too."

"For you? What do you mean?" Dad peers at me behind his glasses.

Keiko's words echo in my head. *I remind myself why I play, what it is I get up onstage for. The audience melts away, and I can play my heart out.*

I finally have an answer for why I want to get up onstage.

It's to prove to myself that I can do it.

"Mom, Dad, I've worked hard to do the things you've asked me to. I get good grades, I've learned Mandarin, and I do my best to respect adults and do what's expected of me."

Mom nods. "Yes, we're so proud of you for being such a good daughter."

I stare at my feet. "But I'm not proud of myself."

My parents' faces immediately fall. "Oh, Lily. Why not?" Dad asks, eyebrows furrowing.

Tears spring to my eyes, and I blink to keep them back. "I never do anything for *me*, because I believe in it or because I want to."

"You don't believe that a good education will help you?" Mom asks.

"Oh, I do," I reassure her. "But doing well in school isn't the only thing I want to do. I want to explore other things, like how to play an electric guitar."

"But where is learning those things going to take you, Lily?" Dad asks. "Do you want to be a musician when you grow up? Is that why this camp is so important to you?"

I shake my head. "I don't know what I want to be. But do I need to know? Can't I . . . experiment? Have fun, be a kid?"

"Is going to the school board something you want to . . . experiment with?" Dad asks.

"Yes. I know it might not work. But at least I would have tried." I think about what Mom said about a good education. "I do believe that a good education will open doors for me. So will exploring talents like drawing and music and acting. Everybody should have a good education. It's unfair that kids who are new to Pacific Park and don't know English don't get to learn and experiment with these things because their English isn't perfect. Vivian deserves to learn about American history, or biology, or English literature. Not reading or writing English very well shouldn't stop her from doing that."

Mom smiles. "That's a solid argument, Lily."

"Plus," I say, softly, "there are other people counting on me, too."

"Other people?" Dad adjusts the glasses on his nose. "Like who?"

"Like my friends, Marcos and Yoona."

It feels really good to say that out loud. Marcos Alvarez and Yoona Kim are my friends.

"Marcos is the boy who called you the other day?" Mom asks.

I blush slightly. "Marcos's family speaks Spanish at home and can't afford extra tutoring. Yoona wants to be a manga artist but can't work on her drawing as much as she wants because she spends so much of her time tutoring Korean kids. If we get ESL classes at Pacific Park Middle, everyone wins. Not only the kids who need tutoring, but the kids who support and care about them, too."

I keep going. "You said it yourself, Dad. You and Mom moved here to give me opportunities I wouldn't have had in Taiwan. The opportunity I want is to speak up when I see something that I think can be done better."

Dad shoots Mom a worried look. But Mom puts her hand on his. "Yes, you're right, Lily. We did come here for the chance to be more free."

She turns to Dad. "Steven, Lily has a good point. We need to give her the freedom she deserves to make her own choices. Even if we don't agree."

"I'm glad you told me more about Taiwan and what's happening there," I add. "I know it was hard for you. I understand where you're coming from." I gulp nervously. "I hope you understand where I'm coming from, too."

"Yes," Mom says softly. "I understand, too."

But Dad's face twists, like he's battling something in his head. He glances toward Ah-ma's door, then back at me and Mom.

After a moment, he speaks. "Okay, Lily. I won't stop you. It does make me nervous, but I understand that it's something you need to do. We'll be there to support you, no matter what."

He opens up his arms, and I rise from the rocking chair and sink into them for an uncharacteristic but much needed Xiao-family hug. Mom pats my hair.

"You're a good girl, Lily," she whispers. "I'm proud of how you're challenging us."

But there's still an elephant in the room.

Or more like a rooster.

"What about Ah-ma?" I sniff. "Is what I'm about to do going to totally freak her out?"

"Oh, Lily," Dad says, pulling back to look me in the eyes. "She's not angry at you. She's scared for you. She'll come around."

I'm not so sure. Will Ah-ma ever be ready to let go of what she's afraid of? Will she ever be comfortable with the idea of her granddaughter speaking up to defend what's right?

"I should tell her what I'm going to do, though. I don't want to hide it from her," I insist.

Dad shakes his head. "We'll handle her. We can't change her, and we shouldn't. She needs to grieve and protect herself the best way she can. But she can't stop you."

"Okay," I say softly.

Later, in my room, I read through the speech that Vivian, Yoona, and Marcos helped me write.

I've never felt prouder of anything in my life. Winning Student of the Year is nothing compared to this.

I can't erase Ah-ma's fear. Those memories are here to stay, no matter how deep she's pushed them down or how painful they feel when they surface again. But I know that behind that fear is a deep love for her family, for me, for Vivian. She's trying to protect us the only way she knows how.

I can show her that things can be different, though.

CHAPTER
31

THE TUESDAY AFTERNOON OF THE board meeting is bright and sunny. I'm standing at the top of the district office's front steps, pulling at the stiff collar of the button-down shirt I'm wearing, pressed glistening white by Mom to make me look as respectable as possible.

I don't mind the outfit, though. It isn't grunge style, but I don't need a grunge outfit to feel powerful and bold.

I'm grunge enough inside.

Vivian's hand is clasped tightly in mine as we lean against the wall. We're both listening to music through my earphones, and my power anthem, Pearl Jam's "Alive," courses through them. Mom, Dad, Auntie, and

Uncle are standing to my right, chatting with Yoona and her parents.

Ah-ma's not here, though. She finally emerged from her room yesterday, but she didn't say anything when I wished her good morning. She just took my bowl of dry cereal away.

A few minutes later, I heard the sound of something sizzling from the kitchen. Soon after, Ah-ma came back with a steaming plate of oyster omelet and a pair of chopsticks.

She only grunted when I thanked her.

Later that night, Dad came into my room and told me that he talked to her about my school board plan. "She's very worried, as expected," he said, smoothing down my hair as he sat next to me on my bed. "But not angry. Let's give her some space to process, okay?"

The only thing I can do is hope Dad is right.

But there was still a part of me that wished Ah-ma would accept my plan and come to this board meeting with the rest of my family. Even though she made me breakfast yesterday, Ah-ma didn't respond when I knocked on her bedroom door to tell her we were leaving. I guess her coming to witness her granddaughter speak up against the "government" was asking too much.

From my perch at the top of the district office stairs,

I see Marcos standing with a crowd of his family members, including his aunt and uncle and cousin, Carlos. I recognize a few other Pacific Park Middle classmates and their families, too, like Trinh Nguyen and Alex Ocampo.

Even Mr. Silvers is here, chatting with a bunch of parents. After class yesterday, I went up to his desk and asked him how ESL classes had worked at Pacific Park Middle before.

"Well, because we didn't have enough teachers who spoke the various languages to offer bilingual support, we grouped English learners by their abilities. Then, once a day, they'd come to a special class and get some focused help from a credentialed teacher," Mr. Silvers explained.

"Okay, thanks, Mr. Silvers. This is good to know," I responded. "I'd like to mention what different kinds of ESL support besides full English immersion could look like at Pacific Park Middle when I go to the school board meeting tomorrow."

"But Lily, why are you going to the school board if you've gathered those signatures already?" he asked, his glasses slightly crooked on his nose. "Didn't you give your petition to Principal Klein?"

"Yes, but Principal Klein called the people who signed it to convince them to support English-only immersion," I told him.

A strange expression fell across his face. But after he

wished me luck, he didn't say anything else.

It's nice that Mr. Silvers showed up today. He might be helpful if I end up needing a real teacher to back me up.

The door to the district office suddenly opens, and an older man with white hair in a green sweater-vest over a brown button-down shirt waves us in. "The board is ready for you all now."

Vivian grins at me and hands me my earphones. I tuck Pearl Jam into my backpack, and we walk in together, hand in hand. We follow the man past a few offices until he gets to the room at the end of the hall-way. "We'll be meeting in the auditorium," he says as he pulls the door open and lets us all through.

At the opposite side of the large room we've just entered is a long line of tables draped with black table-cloths. A mic and placard, each with the name of a board member, are placed in the middle of every table, and seated in black leather chairs are the board members. I count them quickly—there's two women and four men, and the one who opened the front door takes his seat in the middle to make it seven members total.

Along the left wall is a single table, where Ms. Jensen sits with a pad of paper and can of pens in front of her. Rows of folding chairs fill the rest of the room, and in the front, between the rows of chairs and the tables where the board members are sitting, is a podium.

Guess that's where I'll be when it's time.

My heart starts to pound at what feels like rock-music tempo, which the guitar book says is usually between 110 and 140 beats per minute.

Yeah, that feels about right.

We shuffle in and find seats. I head straight to the row closest to the mic, while Vivian takes the seat on my right. Marcos and Yoona join us on my left.

"You got this," Marcos whispers to me, nudging me with his shoulder. Yoona leans over and gives me a double thumbs-up. "Knock 'em dead." She grins.

I smile back with as much confidence as I can muster.

Once the audience settles in, the man in the middle leans forward and speaks into his mic. "Welcome to today's Pacific Park school board meeting. The date is April 13, 1993. I'm Superintendent Mark Walsh, and I will be moderating this meeting. As per our usual protocol, we will first discuss and take votes on pre-agreed-upon agenda items. Then we will open the floor for comments and new topics from the public."

For the next hour, the board runs through agenda items and votes on various things. They discuss a zoning law, approve funds to buy more diverse books for the libraries, and agree to apply for a grant to update the school gyms. There's even a proposal to buy a few computers for the district office.

To my surprise, when the board members ask for comments from the audience about the technology, Dad walks over to the mic.

"My name is Steven Xiao, and I work at CompuScape. I suggest you look into the ThoughtPad 600 for your computing needs. It has one of the most powerful hard drives on the market, which will make everything run much faster." His voice is clear and strong, and he doesn't pull on the collar of his teal polo shirt like he usually does when he's nervous.

A crescendo of pride rises in my body.

My dad's not that predictable, after all.

Superintendent Walsh tells Ms. Jensen to make note of Dad's suggestion and thanks him for speaking up.

As Dad takes his seat three rows behind me, I notice Marcos's aunt and uncle sitting behind them. I remember Marcos telling me that they don't understand much English, which means they probably aren't following what's happening.

It's not fair that adults like them can't participate in forums like this one because they express themselves in a language other than English. It's like a never-ending cycle. How will someone feel like a part of this country if they can't be a part of important conversations that could change their lives?

A wave of bravery hits me for what I'm hoping to do

for their kids, and I sit a little straighter in my chair.

The board finishes the last item on their preapproved agenda, and Superintendent Walsh speaks into his mic again. "We now open the floor for comments from the public. I'd like to remind everyone to speak respectfully and with an open mind. Each person will be given three minutes to speak. Will members of the public with a topic to discuss please approach the mic and speak their case for board consideration?"

That's my cue. It's time to fight for everything I want—ESL classes for Pacific Park Middle students, the chance to go to Camp Rock Out with my best friend, and the right and privilege to stand up for what I believe in.

Robot: initiate SPEAK UP sequence.

CHAPTER
32

VIVIAN SQUEEZES MY HAND ONE last time. Marcos nods at me encouragingly, and Yoona holds her hand up for a high five. I wipe my clammy palms on my skirt and make my way to the podium.

The lights at the front of the room are brighter than I expected, and as I stand in front of the mic, seven pairs of eyes focus on me. Behind me, I feel the audience watching. But because my back is to them, they don't feel quite as scary.

Plus, I know my band is here, supporting me.

I close my eyes for a second. The image of my Pearl Jam poster, with Eddie Vedder crooning into the mic with the intense feeling and commitment he's famous for, flashes into my head. So does Pandora's Box and how incredibly awesome they looked and sounded the first time I saw them practice in Joan's garage.

I even see my ah-gong, standing up many years ago for what he believed in. It's awful that he got punished for it, but we're in America now, in a totally different time and place.

You can do this, Lily.

I take a deep breath and start my speech.

"Dear respected board members. My name is Lily Xiao, and I'm a seventh grader at Pacific Park Middle School and was given the Student of the Year award last year for sixth grade. I'm here representing the voices of the Pacific Park Middle students who are eager, hard-working, and ready to learn, but are held back because of their English language skills."

Superintendent Walsh's eyebrows shoot up, and a few board members shift around in their chairs.

I keep going. "At Pacific Park Middle, those students, like my cousin, Vivian, are on their own, because the school uses full English immersion as the way to teach. But when you're in middle school and there's so much to take in and learn, spending the whole day in English is super hard. Kids miss out on exciting subjects like biology, social studies, or literature, because they can't follow the lesson. Not knowing English holds them back from exploring the subjects that they might fall in love with and want to learn more about as they become adults. It slows them down . . . a lot.

"In the process of learning English, we don't want to lose our connection to our native languages, either. I was born in Pacific Park, and my family is from Taiwan. I can express myself in English and Mandarin, and knowing the two makes me appreciate both my cultures—and where they mix. Full English immersion means we'd need to speak English at home, which would force me and my family to communicate in a language that doesn't come naturally to us. We'd lose our ability to connect with each other and say what's in our minds."

As I speak, I can hear my voice, strong and bold, echoing off the walls and filling the space. That's because today, instead of doubt churning away in my stomach, it's conviction.

Pandora's Box would be so proud.

So would Eddie Vedder and the rest of Pearl Jam.

"Instead of full English immersion, some schools have bilingual programs, where kids learn in their native language and slowly get more and more English exposure. Some have classes where English learners are grouped by ability and a credentialed teacher helps them in a focused, customized way."

In my head, I thank Keiko for telling me about her

Japanese school and Mr. Silvers for telling me about how ESL used to work at Pacific Park Middle.

"I don't know the right way to solve this problem. But what I'm asking for today is that the school board put some time and money into considering different approaches to helping ESL students get the English education they need."

I feel my body tingle for a moment. I believe in every word of this speech, which is making it so I don't veer into robot mode. But there's something else stirring inside me that's trying to come out.

From the chest, through your heart, and out through your voice.

I go off script and let myself say what's on my mind . . . and in my heart.

"Someone said to me once that the best way to learn how to be American is to learn English. But I think being American is about more than that."

I pause, thinking about how my family wasn't allowed to speak up in the way I am. "Being American is about having the permission and privilege to stand up and speak out for what you think is right. That's why I'm in front of the board today. Because I have an opinion that deserves to be heard."

Superintendent Walsh nods his head slowly. So do a few of the other board members.

I keep going. "This opinion isn't only mine. A few of us started a petition and collected over three hundred signatures. There is a lot of support in the Pacific Park community for giving kids more help to learn English."

Superintendent Walsh raises his hand, interrupting me. "Where is this petition, Lily? It'd be helpful to take a look."

Gulp. How am I going to explain what happened with those signatures?

Suddenly, there's a rustle behind me. I turn around to see what's happening. . . .

And it's her. It's Principal Klein, heading up to the podium from the back of the room.

My heart sinks. Again? She's done enough.

But I can't stop her now. So I watch, heart pounding, as she struts up the aisle. She hugs a pile of slightly crumpled papers to her chest, and as she gets closer, I see what they are.

They're our petition pages. What is she planning to do now?

Principal Klein finally joins me at the podium. She clears her throat and speaks into the mic. "The petition papers are here, Superintendent Walsh. I've been . . . uh . . . keeping them safe for the students."

What is going on?

She hands the papers to me, her lips tight. "These are

yours, Lily," she whispers. "I'm sorry. I shouldn't have done what I did."

I'm so confused about what's happening. But I accept the papers anyway. "Thank you, Principal Klein," I whisper in reply.

She turns and leaves me alone at the podium again.

I face the school board and wave the papers in the air. "There are over three hundred signatures from students and adults here. We believe that ESL support is something Pacific Park Middle students deserve. We hope you take our petition into consideration."

"Bring them to me, please," Superintendent Walsh says, and I walk up to the row of tables and hand them to him before taking my place again behind the mic. He flips through them. "Thank you, Lily, for your impassioned speech. This is a very worthwhile topic, and we appreciate you bringing it to our attention."

I beam at him, my heart swelling with pride. I finally did it. I spoke up about something I really believe in. And I did it with all the emotion and feeling in my soul.

He continues. "Because ESL support is a new topic that's being presented today, the board will not be voting on it immediately. We need to do our due diligence to better understand the issue, then add it to a future agenda to allow more members of the public to comment. After that, we'll be able to vote. It's April now, and I anticipate that we will be able to move forward on a decision by the last meeting of this school year, in June."

June? My heart sinks. Behind me, I hear a titter of voices whispering.

June is *forever* from now.

At this rate, the due date for Vivian's Evergreen transfer decision is going to come and go before we know if Pacific Park Middle will have ESL support next year. Not to mention registering for Camp Rock Out by this Friday.

"Would it be possible to vote on this sooner, Superintendent Walsh? Students need help now." I try to hide the desperation creeping into my voice.

He binds the papers together with a big paperclip and places them on the table. "We have official procedures we have to follow. But your collection of petitions gives us a strong sense of what the community wants. We'll do our best to expedite a proposal and vote on next steps."

"With that, your three minutes are up, Lily." He turns toward the audience. "Next public topic, please."

I step away from the mic and slowly shuffle back to my seat. Marcos throws me a double thumbs-up, and Yoona squeezes my arm as I pass. When I sit back down next to Vivian, she nudges my elbow and whispers, "Thank you, biǎo jiě. For standing up for me. For all of us." She motions at the rows of family and friends behind us.

I smile weakly at her and squeeze her hand back.

I'm a whirlwind of emotions. Although it was nerve-racking, it was amazing to get up in front of an audience, speak into a real mic, and have my voice come out strong and passionate and full of feeling for the first time ever.

My voice didn't sound anything like Eddie's. Or Joan's. That's okay, though. What matters is that it's mine.

But the board won't decide anything for another two months—long after registration for Camp Rock Out is over and Auntie and Uncle have to decide on Evergreen Prep. Vivian will definitely get the English support she needs there. But at Pacific Park Middle, it's a toss-up.

Goodbye, fun summer of grunge rock goodness.

And goodbye, having my cousin by my side.

CHAPTER
33

AFTER SUPERINTENDENT WALSH adjourns the meeting, we quietly make our way outside. It's early evening, and the sun is shining its last perfect rays over Pacific Park, making the shadows stretch long against the ground.

Yoona tackles me with a bear hug. "That was fantastic, Lily!" she squeals. "Your speech was great—it went like we planned. I teared up listening to you!"

"Totally." Marcos bumps my shoulder with his. "The Student of the Year delivers!"

Despite my disappointment, I can't help but smile proudly back. "Yeah, I didn't do that bad, did I?"

"You do perfect, biǎo jiě! I'm so proud of you!" Vivian says in English, bouncing up and down in excitement.

"It's going to take a while for them to make a decision, though." I look down and kick at a pebble in frustration. "They won't decide in time for Camp Rock Out registration. Those forms are due in three days. And what about Evergreen Prep?"

Vivian shrugs. "Wǒ bù zhī dào, Lily," she says, switching to Chinese. "It's up to my parents now. I guess I'll probably have to transfer schools."

But she brightens up. "It's okay, though. What's important is that you've helped other kids, too. I'm sure the board will approve the funding, especially after they see how many signatures you got." She beams at me assuredly.

Marcos and Yoona look between me and Vivian with soft, patient faces, and I quickly translate what Vivian said.

"Yeah!" Yoona affirms. "The school district now knows how much the community cares about this. I know you wanted everything to happen faster, but sometimes, the first step is the most important one. Today was a huge one."

Marcos chimes in. "Yeah, good thing we got those signatures first. It sounds like that'll speed up the decision. Can you believe that Principal Klein showed up the way she did? I wonder what changed her mind?"

"That was my doing," a familiar voice says from behind us.

We spin around. It's Mr. Silvers.

"You made her give us our petition papers back?" Marcos's eyes go big, his long lashes making them seem even bigger.

Mr. Silvers nods. "After Lily told me what Principal Klein did with the signatures you'd collected, I couldn't stand on the sidelines anymore. I should have said something sooner and fought harder for school resources once I saw so many students come through my class who needed extra help with English."

Mr. Silvers continues. "I'm a teacher, and my responsibility is to the students. The three of you made more progress than I did, which is fantastic. But I should have done more, too." He smooths down his sweater-vest and pushes his glasses up his nose. "I had a long meeting with Principal Klein yesterday. She's still not convinced that ESL classes are the best approach. But I helped her see that you students have the right to raise the issues you care about, and that she should have let you do that. That's why she showed up today."

Looks like Principal Klein isn't totally on our side . . . yet. And the things she's said to me before, about how immigrants need to work harder at adopting American culture and how Asians like me and Yoona are always smart, still make me angry.

But at least she did the right thing today and let us give our petition to the school board. It's a small step . . .

and although I wish it were much bigger, it's something.

I scan the crowd milling around, and I spot Principal Klein off to the side. Our eyes meet, and she holds my gaze. Then she gives me a slight nod before walking away.

I face Mr. Silvers again. "Thank you, Mr. Silvers," I say softly, "for believing in us."

He squeezes my shoulder. "I'll work with Principal Klein and the board to plan next steps, and I'll call you and your families when we're ready to discuss this again with the community. Congratulations to the three of you." He waves goodbye and heads toward the parking lot.

I think English lit is going to be one of my favorite classes now on account of my new favorite teacher.

Mom, Dad, Auntie, and Uncle join us, and Dad puts up his hand for a high five. "Hey, hey, gong xǐ, Lily! That was a wonderful speech," he cheers in Mandarin.

Mom gives me a big hug. "Lily, I saw a side of you that I'd never seen before. You spoke with such . . . feeling. You were utterly convincing. I love this new you."

Auntie chimes in, too. "That speech was worthy of the podium, I'd say! What a fascinating process, too, this way of engaging with the community."

"Hey, Lily, I'm gonna bounce." Marcos drops his skateboard down on the concrete sidewalk and places a sneakered foot on it. "My people are waiting." He tips his head in the direction of the parking lot, and sure enough, I see his family glance our way.

"Yeah, me too," Yoona adds. "By the way, this is for you." She rips a page out of the sketchbook she's hugging and hands it to me.

It's me represented in manga style, like her last drawing. This time, Yoona's drawn me tall and proud and standing on a stage with a mic in my hands, crooning into it like Eddie Vedder would. The board members are in the audience, their fists in the air.

Wow. I look like a real grunge rocker performing at a concert.

"Thought you might like to get a sense of your vibe up there." Yoona grins. Then she and Marcos peel away and join their respective families.

As I watch them walk away, I smile to myself.

Yeah, I'm pretty sure I have real friends now.

"Come on, let's head home." Dad tousles my hair. "You must be exhausted."

Mom loops her arms around mine and leads the six of us toward our white Volvo. Auntie and Uncle's green Subaru is parked right next to it. "Why doesn't everyone come over tonight, and we'll whip up something simple for dinner? We don't have much at home but noodles, but we should do something to celebrate this big step that Lily made today for Vivian and the family."

Auntie and Uncle agree, and we pile into our respective cars and head to our place.

But when we walk through the front door, a surprise greets us. The dining table is covered with a sea of small plates with pieces of raw meats, seafood, vegetables, and noodles on them. Our trusty hot pot bubbles in the middle.

Ah-ma comes out of the kitchen, wiping her hands on her flowered apron.

"Jìn lái, jìn lái!" She ushers us in, motioning Auntie, Uncle, and Vivian toward their usual set of guest slippers. Mine, Dad's, and Mom's have been laid out as well.

"Ma, what are you up to?" Dad asks, his voice loaded with the surprise I'm feeling, too.

"I'm preparing a nice dinner for my family," Ah-ma replies in Taiwanese. "And for our brave Lily, of course." She reaches out to pat my cheek, like she's done a million times. But for a split second, she hesitates, like she's afraid of my reaction. . . .

I grab her hand and squeeze it tight as my heart grows about a thousand times bigger. "All this for me, Ah-ma?" I ask incredulously.

Ah-ma lets out a short breath and guides me to the dining table. She sits me at the head of the table, where she usually sits, and picks up and places chopsticks in my hand. "Come, tsa-bóo-sun. Let's eat."

I don't need to hear Ah-ma say how proud she is of me for what I did today. And that she's trying hard to understand and accept what I've done and why.

Her actions show me loud and clear.

We sit down to dinner, and Dad gives Ah-ma the rundown of what happened at the board meeting.

"The principal came?" Ah-ma asks, her updo jiggling as she glances my way. "Even after she called all those people to tell them not to sign the . . . what is it called again? Petition?"

"Isn't that amazing?" Mom exclaimed. "Totally unexpected."

I shake my head to stop the praise. "It was good that she showed up and gave us our petition back, but she still thinks that English immersion is the right way to go. Honestly, I think she came more so she wouldn't get in trouble for squashing a student petition than because she actually cares. But maybe this small step will lead to bigger, bolder ones down the line."

Ah-ma smiles at me. "Good girl for at least sparking a change." She pauses, her face turning sad yet hopeful for a moment. "I think your ah-gong would have been proud of you today," she whispers.

I swallow down the ball of sadness that's come up my throat at the thought of my ah-gong and what he tried to do. "Thanks, Ah-ma. I'm glad that we're in a place where we can speak up without being afraid." I squeeze her hand.

Ah-ma turns to Auntie and Uncle. "What now?" she asks. "Will you still send Vivian to Evergreen?"

My heart beats in triple time. Here it is.

Vivian glances at me nervously.

Auntie and Uncle exchange looks, and Auntie puts her chopsticks down. "We talked last night about the different scenarios that might happen as a result of Lily's petition. We decided that if there wasn't a decision made today, we're going to cross our fingers and hope that it'll be a yes. Vivian can stay at Pacific Park Middle."

"Woo-hoo!" Vivian and I both cheer, and a huge wave of relief rolls over me.

"But what if the board says no?" Mom says, her eyebrows wrinkled with concern. "Vivian will be back where she started."

"We can use some of the money we had earmarked for Evergreen to get Vivian more specialized tutoring for eighth grade. It won't be as much as what Evergreen or Pacific Park Middle could provide, but it's something." Auntie reaches out and tucks a strand of Vivian's hair behind her ear. "I'm sorry, but we'll need to save the money for this summer camp you want to go to. In case those ESL classes don't come through."

Gulp. Guess it's final. No Vivian at Camp Rock Out. I try to push down the disappointment churning in my stomach.

"Well, I have some important news, too," Dad suddenly volunteers, a big smile on his face. "After I got feedback about me not demonstrating enough initiative to be promoted, I decided to share my idea with another team at CompuScape."

"Wow, you did? What happened?" Uncle asks.

"Wait!" I blurt out. Despite how bummed I'm feeling about Camp Rock Out, Dad deserves an exciting setup for what sounds like some good news. I turn to Vivian. "Hey, biǎo mèi, set the stage for my dad."

She grabs a pair of clean chopsticks and taps them against the table in an impressive drumroll. When she's done, I flash Dad a thumbs-up. "Take it away, Dad!"

He laughs. "They loved my idea, and I'll be switching teams. I'm getting a promotion after all."

"Dad, that's so great," I breathe out. "Congratulations!"

"I guess it does pay off to rock the boat a bit," he says, winking at me.

I'm happy that my super predictable dad has figured out how to speak up in his own way. At least *he* got what he wanted.

Mom beams proudly. "There's more. Because of

Steven's promotion, he's gotten a raise, which means we have more spending money. We'd like to pay for both Vivian and Lily to go to the rock camp."

My heart leaps into my throat as Auntie's mouth drops open. "Oh, no, we can't accept that!" she exclaims.

"We insist," Dad chimes in. "This is a gift for Lily, for how brave she's been today. I know how badly she's been wanting to go with Vivian, so we want to make that happen for the two of you."

I clap my hands in excitement and beam at my parents. My grin is so big I'm sure it's about to stretch out my face permanently. "Thank you so much, Mom and Dad! Vivian, we did it! You and me, rocking out at Camp Rock Out together—it's what we've always wanted."

But hearing those words come out of my mouth makes me pause, and I glance over at Vivian. She's looking back at me with what seems like a big, excited expression on her face, but something in her eyes doesn't look quite right.

When Vivian and I were fighting over the phone, I said the exact same thing, that Camp Rock Out was what we both wanted. Vivian had shouted back that I was being selfish, and that I wasn't thinking about what she wanted or what she needed.

It's true that going to Camp Rock Out with Vivian this summer has been *my* dream this whole time. Even though Vivian does like grunge music, it's always me leading the charge, me who loves going to Power Records after school, who thought of asking Keiko for help, who made the deal to exchange good grades for the chance to go to camp. It was me who stepped up to the mic.

And I can't deny that a huge part of wanting Vivian at camp with me was so I wouldn't have to do this scary new thing alone. Her being by my side was about making me less scared, about *my* fear of being the one girl in a sea of skater boys.

All that has been about me, *my* dreams, *my* fears. It hasn't been about Vivian, about what my biǎo mèi really wants. And what she really needs.

Vivian's right. I have been selfish. I have been a chicken.

"Hey, biǎo mèi?" I say.

"Yeah?"

"You know how much I want you to come to Camp Rock Out with me. We'd have so much fun, with you on drums and me on guitar." I take a deep breath. "But if you feel like you need it, maybe you should start on your English tutoring now, instead of waiting for the new school year to begin. Mom, Dad, could Vivian use the money to go to bǔ xí bān this summer instead?"

They nod. "Yes, of course. We'd be supportive of that."

Vivian's eyes widen in a way that makes her look like

Xiǎo Dīng Dāng. "But I don't want to leave you without a drummer. You'd be alone!"

I smile at her reassuringly. "I'll be okay. Because you were right. I haven't been thinking about you and what you want and need. You need to do what's best for you. I can go to Camp Rock Out on my own. It'll be scary, but I can do it. I'm not afraid to make new friends anymore. And you can still be my drummer!"

Ah-ma grins. "That's great, Lily. You're doing a wonderful job watching out for your biǎo mèi."

"That's very generous of you, Lily," Auntie adds. "Vivian, I'll let you decide what you'd like to do."

Vivian nods. "Okay, thanks. I'll think about it."

She fishes a piece of shrimp out of the hot pot and puts it in my bowl. "Remember, the head's the best part," she says, grinning.

I look at my family chatting away with each other over Ah-ma's delicious hot pot. We've each grown up in worlds very far apart, and those experiences have made us who we are today, with our fears, our hopes, our dreams.

Now, we're here together in a safe, supportive place that gives us the permission to speak up when we see something that's not right, that's unfair. And to demand change that makes it better.

When I got up onstage today, I didn't have an electric

guitar in my arms, and Vivian wasn't behind me with drumsticks in her hands.

But I had something I wanted to tell the world, and I had the guts to speak out.

Turns out I don't need to go to a grunge rock camp to transform. That passion and power was in me the whole time.

I just needed the right message to unlock it.

Robot: get ready to rock out.

EPILOGUE

FROM STAGE LEFT, I POKE my head around the curtains to peek at the audience. Even though most of the lights are angled toward the stage where I'm standing, I can tell it's a full house. Kids, parents, and other people from the Pacific Park community are up on their feet, jumping up and down to Pandora's Box's high-energy performance.

Joan's belting her heart out into a mic while Keiko jams on the guitar, her hair up in her usual buns but styled with cool-looking spikes coming out of them. Tori's curly hair flies as her hands move in a blur at the drums, and Maia stands like a statue, her bass churning out distorted riffs and rhythms.

Meanwhile, Marcos and I nervously wait offstage

with the rest of our band members for our turn to get onstage after Pandora's Box finishes their opening act.

It's finally time for our big moment—the end-of-camp performance that will bring together everything we've learned at Camp Rock Out over the past month.

I'm not going to lie—rock camp hasn't been easy. I've gone home more than a few times with a hoarse throat, callused fingers, a sore neck, and aching shoulders.

But it's also been amazingly energizing and eye-opening. I've learned tons of cool stuff, like how to tune my own guitar, how to play more power chords, and how to adjust gain and overdrive settings on the amp to get that rich rock sound.

On top of the techniques, I'm also starting to settle into a more natural, fluid way of playing. With so much practice, my brain doesn't have to think so hard about where my fingers need to go anymore, and I can focus on getting the emotion and feelings out.

After all this work, it's time to finally show the world what I can do.

I bump Marcos's shoulder with mine. "Are you ready for this?" I shout.

Instead of his backward green baseball cap today, Marcos is wearing a red one with our band logo stitched on it. He's paired the band T-shirt that Yoona designed for us with his usual baggy jeans. As for me, I've got my ponytail tied up high, so I can really whip it back and forth when I get into it. Over my band T-shirt is my trusty red-and-black flannel shirt, and I'm wearing black jeans and my not-so-new-anymore black patent leather boots.

But what strikes me as strange right now isn't the red instead of green cap on Marcos's head. It's the expression on his face, twisted and strange.

"Uh-oh, what's wrong?" I ask, concerned. "Everything okay? We're going to be on soon."

"When I'm nervous, my stomach growls." Marcos shakes his head, face reddening. He adjusts the guitar strap over his shoulder and rubs his belly. "It'll go away once I start playing."

His face lights up. "By the way, speaking of food, can you hook me up with more of your grandma's sticky dumplings? And those green onion pancakes? They are sooo good!"

"Totally!" I grin.

After the school board meeting, Ah-ma told us that she wanted to spend more time out of the house so she could learn how to be independent and not rely on us so much. She started playing mahjong with Auntie Ying a lot more at the church.

Then a funny thing happened. Auntie Ying came up with the idea to expand her business by also offering

Ah-ma's homemade bah-oâns. That way, people could order both with one phone call. I even gave Marcos and his family some at the beginning of summer. Now Ah-ma's more than busy cooking and hanging out at Auntie Ying's house a few times a week to fulfill orders.

Suddenly, I spot Ah-ma's rooster updo bobbing up and down among the campers hanging out backstage. Vivian's with her, too, looking around bewilderedly.

"Hey, over here!" I wave at them. They push their way through the chaos.

When they reach me, Vivian's breathless and laughing, while Ah-ma seems a bit nervous about the flurry of activity around her.

"Hey, biǎo jiě! Wow, the energy back here is amazing," Vivian yells, trying to be heard above Keiko's guitar solo.

"Isn't it?" I shout back. "Hopefully you'll get to join us next summer!" I take Ah-ma's arm and loop it around mine, patting it softly. She smiles back at me, her face settling into something a bit more at ease.

Vivian decided not to do Camp Rock Out after all. Even though the school board voted in June to fund ESL classes at Pacific Park Middle next school year, Vivian thought it was best that she got a head start with some extra English help over the summer.

I was a bit sad when she told me, but I knew it was the

right thing for her. We agreed that once Camp Rock Out is over, I'll teach her what I've learned so we can still practice together.

"Before you go on, we want to give you some presents," Vivian says, bouncing up and down on her toes in excitement. "I have the first one, and everyone chipped in—Mom, Dad, Ah-ma, and your parents."

"Aw, that's so nice, biǎo mèi!" I exclaim.

She hands me a small plastic box, and I pull open the lid slowly . . .

. . . and inside is a colorful mix of different types of guitar picks.

"Wow, cool!" I exclaim. "I've never seen such fancy picks before!"

"Look closer, biǎo jiě," Vivian urges me.

I hold one up to the stage lights, and there's gold lettering engraved on it. I squint to read it . . .

. . . and the words say "Lily Xiao, Grunge Rocker."

Tears well up in my eyes, and I blink quickly to stop them.

My family finally gets it.

"My turn now," Ah-ma says, handing me another small box. This one is made of dark wood and is smooth to the touch.

I crack it open. Resting on top of its soft, velvety lining is another guitar pick. But this one's older, more worn, like it'd been used a lot before.

Ah-ma doesn't yell to be heard over the loud music. Instead, she pulls me in closer so she can speak into my ear. "This belonged to your ah-gong. I've saved it all these years . . . and now, it's yours."

This time, I can't stop the tears running down my face. I wipe them with the back of my hand and give both Ah-ma and Vivian a big hug.

"To-siā," I manage to say in Taiwanese.

Vivian beams back at me. "We're so excited to hear you play. By the way, I invited Mai Sok and Grace Lopez, too. Hope that's okay."

"Oh, totally. The more the merrier!"

Vivian's been making friends at her English tutoring class, which has been super fun to see. Because they get where each other is coming from, they're not so shy when speaking in English with each other.

I'm so glad Vivian's got her own friends. Because I know that at the end of the day, no matter how many new friends we make, we'll always have each other.

"All right, we better get back," Vivian finally says, and after one last hug, I wave as they disappear back into the melee of campers.

A few minutes later, Pandora's Box ends their set with a huge bang, and the audience cheers and whoops. The band members take their bows and head offstage in a flurry. Keiko spots me, strands of hair plastered on her cheeks.

She stops to squeeze my shoulder. "Knock 'em dead, Lily. And remember, it's not about perfection . . . it's about the passion and feeling in your heart!" she calls out breathlessly. Then she follows the rest of her bandmates offstage.

Right, I tell my churning stomach, which is probably growling as loud as Marcos's is.

I need to remember what I'm getting up onstage for.

Kurt, one of the Camp Rock Out counselors, walks up to the mic. "That was Pacific Park's very own Pandora's Box, our opening act. And now, the moment you've been waiting for—it's time for our campers to play the pieces they've been practicing for us!"

My heart starts to thump, and I breathe in and out to calm my nerves.

"Up first is the Rockin' Robots, featuring Lily Xiao on vocals and lead guitar, Marcos Alvarez on bass, Eric Smith on rhythm, and Courtney Jones on percussion! Let's give them a round of applause!"

The audience erupts into a din of noise as they welcome us onstage.

This is it.

Marcos and I grin at each other and make our way under the bright lights, him with his bass strapped across his chest and me with the Camp Rock Out one across mine. Luckily, Yoona designed our band T-shirts in a way that you can see her awesome design of manga-style robots jamming out to rock music no matter how we hold our instruments.

I was the one who came up with the idea of Rockin' Robots for our band name, and luckily, everyone loved it. Because what's wrong with some robotness, anyway? It's hard work and focus that's gotten me to where I am, and it's what will get me to where I will eventually go— as a musician, as a straight-A student . . . maybe even as a skateboarder one day.

I just need to make sure I know which program to pull out when—robot sometimes, rocker sometimes.

Right now, it's grunge rocker time.

I walk up to the mic and hold my hands in position on my guitar.

The spotlights are blinding, but after I blink a few times, my eyes adjust quickly. To my surprise, my entire family is right up in the front row—Dad, Mom, Auntie, Uncle, Ah-ma, and Vivian, along with her new friends.

Instead of his usual blue polo shirt, Dad's wearing one of our Rockin' Robots shirts. When he catches my eye, he cups his hands over his mouth and yells the loudest I've ever heard him shout. "Jiā yóu, Lily!"

Next to him, Mom pumps her hands in the air. "Go, Lily!"

Then I notice that Vivian's got chopsticks in her hands, and she raises them over her head and bangs them together, like drumsticks.

I laugh out loud and bow slightly at my cheering family. I throw my shoulders back, hold my head up high, and hug the guitar closer to my body. I turn to the band. "Ready?" I call out.

To my right, Marcos nods.

I start with a slide of the strings and go straight into the A power chord that kicks off Pearl Jam's "Alive." After a few riffs, Marcos's and Eric's bass and rhythm guitars join me, and Courtney's percussion pumps up the volume.

I feel the stirrings of my conviction and my right to stand up and speak out travel from deep within my chest, through my heart, and out through my mouth. . . .

And the entire auditorium echoes with the power of my voice.

I don't sound like Eddie Vedder. I don't sound like Joan, either.

I'm Lily Xiao, and the music I'm playing sounds different from what's been done before.

But it's familiar at the same time, because it's got the same power and passion as those who've come before me. People like my ah-gong, whose bravery and sacrifice I feel deep in my heart as I launch into the chorus and croon over and over again that I'm still alive.

Together with my new bandmates jamming behind me and my entire family cheering me on, I speak out.

AUTHOR'S NOTE

IN CASE IT'S NOT OBVIOUS, I grew up in the 1990s and loved the grunge and alternative rock music that was so popular then. But choosing to write Lily's story in this time period wasn't just about me reliving the nostalgia of my childhood. I wanted to *rewrite* my youth, to imagine living in the 1990s again as a twelve-year-old, but with the cultural awareness and sensitivities that have evolved since then. That's how— and why—this book was born.

Like Lily, I was a shy, quiet middle schooler without a lot of friends. I did love listening to rock music alone in my room, but it never crossed my mind that a puny, scrawny, Asian American kid with big dorky glasses like me could play an electric guitar. If I had seen someone like Keiko up on a rock-and-roll stage, however, proving to the world that *it is possible*, maybe I would have felt differently. Maybe instead of writing children's books right now, I'd be writing song lyrics and prepping for my next world tour! And so I created Keiko's character to show why diverse representation in media and culture is so impactful to the forming of a young person's dreams and ambitions. I hope Lily's journey to becoming a rocker in the face of what people expected of her (or maybe more accurately, didn't expect of her) inspires you, dear reader, to imagine the wide breadth of identities that you too can hold.

While I felt nearly socially invisible at school, I was relatively well-known for my academic achievements (at the end of sixth grade, my school offered two awards that came with a cash prize. Guess who won both?). But looking back, I think I could have done more with the privilege I had earned as a star student to make significant change happen in my community. The battle for fair and just education for English learners was very real in the 1980s and 1990s, with massive immigration into my home state of California from places like Mexico, China, the Philippines, Vietnam, El Salvador, India, Korea, and Taiwan. The common thinking at the time was to reject an immigrant's native language and have them completely adopt English so they could assimilate as quickly as possible. But we should never be asked to give up parts of ourselves and our heritage in order to integrate into the mainstream. While I was born and raised in the US with English as my native tongue, my parents had the foresight to insist their kids learn Mandarin Chinese. I'm so grateful that they did, even though I protested spending every Friday night at Chinese school! And so, with my teenage privilege as a bilingual top student, I could have been as brave and thoughtful and vocal as Lily is in the face of people who wrongly believe that one's ability to learn a second language has anything to do with their intelligence and humanity. Lily does with her power and pride what I didn't start doing until I was an adult—and I hope you readers acknowledge and use your own power and privilege to fight when you see something that demands change and attention, too.

Finally, I wish I'd had more empathy for my parents and the struggles they underwent as new immigrants. I now understand why they didn't sign up for the PTA, didn't show up at school board meetings, or didn't fight back every time someone questioned their legitimacy as Americans. They chose their battles carefully and fought the ones that'd give their kids more opportunity, not the ones that'd affirm or defend their identities. They didn't have that luxury—but I do, because of the sacrifices they made. That's why I've taken up the mission to write stories that feature proud, joyful Asian Americans who belong. And I hope that the battles I've chosen to fight as a parent give my daughter opportunities I didn't have, so that when she finds her own voice, she has the luxury and power to use it to shout from the rooftops.

And so, if you've read this far, my message to you is this: Don't wait until you're an adult to find your voice (and if you're an adult, it's not too late!). Challenge authority, demand justice, and fight for what you believe in now, because you can, and you should. There is a powerful rocker inside each and every one of you, and I hope with all the beats of my heart—or those of a loud percussion riff—that when you see something in the world that needs changing, you have the courage to stand up to the mic and speak out for everyone to hear.

ACKNOWLEDGMENTS

SOME SAY THAT YOUR SECOND novel is much harder to write than your first, and this was certainly the case for me. And so I'm all the more grateful for the community around me that's helped shepherd Lily's story to life.

Jamie Weiss Chilton, my amazing agent, thank you for your relentless support in nurturing my growing career as a children's book author. You strike a perfect balance between being able to coax forth my best creative self while educating me on the practicalities of the industry, and for all your thoughtfulness and tact, I'm eternally thankful.

To my editor, Jen Ung, you made the experience of editing and publishing my first novel so delightful and rewarding that I had to come back for more! Finding the true anchor of this story took more trial and error than I expected, but your insightful direction made that true north clear in the blink of your expert eye. Thank you for having the faith and trust in me to mold this story into what it needed to be.

Jody Tseng, you brought Lily and her band of activists to life so wonderfully through your enchanting illustrations. Celeste Knudsen, your art and design direction captures the energy and the era of the story so perfectly. Thank you both for taking my words and giving them such bright, visual energy.

There are so many people whose work touches a book in order to get it out into the world, and I'm grateful for the Quill Tree Books and HarperCollins teams for all you do. From copyediting to design to production to marketing and sales and publicity, thank you all so much for believing in this story and working so tirelessly to get it into the hands of young readers around the world.

To my own merry band of writing partners, Belen Medina, Sana Rafi, and Jenny Liao, thank you for your tireless camaraderie as we navigate this intensely rewarding, yet at times opaque (and slow-moving), world of children's book publishing together. When first stories are mere seeds of ideas, they are at their most vulnerable. Yet I trust no one but you three to treat my early drafts with the delicate care, love, and hard truths that they need in order to grow into the stories they were meant to be.

To my parents—when I started to dig into this project and ask you what it was like as young immigrant parents, it was so eye-opening to hear about your lives in Taiwan as children and what it was like when you first came to the US. I didn't know anything about modern Taiwanese history, and it was surprising to me to hear that you also didn't know much about it until you were both out of the then-government's tight grasp of history erasure and silence. Your stories are emblazoned in my mind now, and I promise that one day, they will make their way out of the darkness and into the light through the printed page.

Alex and Kaia, I'm thankful I get to spend every day of my life with you, now and in the future. Without the many meals cooked, the many cuddles given, your never-ending words of encouragement and the permission you both give me to clock out in my role as partner and parent and clock in to my passion as an author, I could never do any of this. So thank you, thank you, thank you.

As I mentioned in my author's note, I wasn't the most perceptive teenager back in the early nineties. So when I first saw the girls who'd later become The Donnas play punk rock at my middle school's talent show, I shrugged them off as a bit strange and unconventional. But when I look back at my childhood and the things that stuck in my subconsciousness, your creativity has sat with me all these years. I now realize how brave it was for you to do what you did. For that, I acknowledge and want to express my respect for you rocker girls.

And finally, to all the Asian American writers who have come before me—like what Keiko meant to Lily and what Lily will hopefully mean for the next generation of Asian American rockers, you and your books showed me that someone like me *can* write and publish books that feature strong, unabashedly proud Asian American kids. I'm so honored to see my books next to yours, and I'm grateful for the privilege to work alongside you as we show kids that a life of creativity and pride as Asian Americans with something important to say and the courage to say it is not only possible, but essential. Thank you.